Border Memories

Edward Matthews

Watermark Press

Published in UK by Watermark Press 2022

A CIP catalogue record for this book is available from the British Library

ISBN: 978-1-8380043-3-0

Typeset in Book Antigua

Cover design by nb-design.com

Printed by Imprint Digital

Watermark Press
Unit 77 Penn Street, Duo Tower, London, England, N1 5FF
www.watermarkpress.co.uk

Contents

CHAPTER 1

I passed a gardener trimming hedges near the lawn-bowling field of Balboa Park where I lingered between appointments. He stopped trimming for a moment, and we made eye contact long enough to know that we recognized each other, but neither of us could recall how, so he continued trimming and I kept walking. I'd grown accustomed to these intrusive memories of people I've never met, places I've never been—other people's memories or some fusion between theirs and mine. The simple part of curating memories was that all of my clients were scheduled for me, I merely showed up; the complex part involved managing expectations, for even the best memories I embedded rarely satiated my clients' desire. Memories are like tattoos in that way—getting the first just leads to more.

My new client lived on the second floor of a charcoal-black building in a portion of Bankers Hill that has—despite repeated real estate conglomerate attempts—resisted being levelled and replaced with apartment complexes that are always either garish or nondescript. This neighborhood had Dutch houses with triangular roofs painted green and red beside modern, geometric houses that Frank Lloyd Wright would've salivated over. Audis and BMWs were parked parallel in front of the complex, tires a perfect three inches from the curb. An iron, key-coded gate surrounded the complex. I pressed the button for number five and the door opened a few seconds later with a click. Outdoor furniture huddled around a firepit in the courtyard. A security guard leaned against the staircase, one leg tucked under the other, swiping at a dating app. A housekeeper answered the doorbell and let me in, my entrance corresponding with the exit of a suited man carrying yard signs with some candidate's name. A wooden cane leaned against the banister next to a pair of leather shoes. The housekeeper pointed up the stairs. The stairwell's wall had framed photos of the same man shaking hands with various politicians I vaguely recognized, the handshaker's hair receding and graying with each photo.

I ascended the last stair and saw the man from the photos sitting in a chair in the corner diagonal to me. The white carpet was vacuumed vertically in some places and horizontally in others, suggesting two housekeepers with divergent directional tastes. A bookcase took up most of the wall to my right, each of the books tightly packed, some with leather binding and gold lettering probably indicating first editions; his reflection shown in the floor-to-ceiling window that took up the park-facing wall as night settled in.

"Take a seat, take a seat."

His shirt stretched tight around his stomach, buttons misaligned with their holes. I looked around the room, registering each of the doors and the exit behind me. A taxidermy buffalo head ornamented the wall opposite where the man sat; its black-marbled eyes like the little cameras you see everywhere.

"Let me ask you something," he paused, "would you rather lose your vision, your legs, or your memory?"

I feigned consideration, tilting my head. I was used to eccentric clients.

"That is an interesting question."

This was my default response to unexpected questions. His face crinkled as if tasting mayonnaise when expecting whipped cream.

He uncapped a Diet Coke and poured it into a mug.

"That's not an answer, darling. Which would it be? Memory, vision, or legs?"

He got up, adjusted his khakis, and sat beside me on the couch, leaning forward with his elbows on his knees as if sharing a secret beside a campfire.

"They sound equally undesirable."

"It's simply a matter of what you value. Do you value your past the most? Or, perhaps, you value your sight the most? Or do you value your movement?" he said, smiling, crow's feet creasing the skin around his eyes.

"Let me put it this way." He pointed to a wooden door beside the bookcase. "Behind that door is a man who will blind you." Then he pointed toward the door beside it, which led, I assume, to the neighboring room. The door knob had an hourglass sculpted onto it. "Behind that door is a man who will wipe your memory." He gestured toward the staircase I ascended earlier. "Waiting at the front door is a man who will paralyze you."

The doors acquired a weight they'd lacked before, as if the mere suggestion of harm increased the probability of its manifestation. I stared at the second door veiled in darkness long enough for my peripherals to dissipate.

"So—which door will it be?"

"The second door."

"Memory. You choose that one every time—why?"

His mannerisms were precise. Even his leisurely movements, like leaning his head back to get the last sip of Diet Coke before refilling the mug, seemed pointedly casual as if imitating someone relaxing.

"Your memory's not valuable to you?" he said, eyebrows arching. "Is there something you'd rather forget?"

I thought of the email I received from my father about what

happened to my brother, but rather than tell this client, I acquiesced to his line of questioning.

"I don't know."

"Ah, I think you do, but you never tell me. You never, *ever* tell me," he said, motioning to the door with the hourglass knob. "Although, you're here to reopen that door for me, aren't you darling?"

"May I ask what you mean?"

"You'll figure it out eventually. You always do."

Footfalls pounded the floor above and Mr. Bray stood and shuffled over to the bookcase, feeling along the wall until his fingers closed around a long-handled broom from where it was leaning, rapping it against the roof. The footfalls ceased.

"I'm going to rent out that fucking apartment just so it can remain empty. I will not keep putting up with this."

He leaned the broom back where it had been, beside a shelf that held what looked to be Native American pottery. He returned to the couch beside me and placed a hand on my shoulder. We sat quiet for an uncomfortable amount of time.

"It is good to make your acquaintance, sir," I said, trying to dispel the quiet.

He smiled gradually, like a Venus flytrap opening after devouring a fly. This look remained unbroken across his face. He nodded to a question he asked himself in his head and sipped the Diet Coke from his mug, wiping his mouth afterward, still in some form of reverie. Instead of family photos on the coffee table, Mr. Bray had what looked like IOU's and stacks of vouchers from cruises and airlines.

"There's a memory I need to acquire," he said.

"What specifically, if I may ask?"

He pressed his thumb into my shoulder as if pinning an assertion to it.

"All you need to know is what I tell you."

I said nothing, hoping he would continue and I could deduce the narrative from the details he gave. Questions seemed to be time-prohibitive with Mr. Bray.

"In Tijuana, there's a girl with a memory I need. Go and get it."

"I would need to verify with my superior."

"You do that."

"It is unlikely, because it runs counter to our Standard Operating Procedure."

"Let me ask you a question: when does a child become a man?"

"I don't know."

"You don't know."

"That is correct. I have not thought about this before."

"You might do well to, darling, you might do well to think about this. Can I give you my answer for when a child becomes a man?"

"Of course."

I defaulted to the script I always followed with my clients—if they asked you to do something, the answer was always yes. If they wanted to tell tangential stories or recount career highlights, I would be their captive audience—not just with my words, but with my mannerisms—nodding at the right moments and expressing the emotion the story elicited at the crucial points. I usually sprinkled in some ego-endorsing comments.

"It takes a ritual. A rite of passage. An initiation. My favorite comes from the Algonquin tribe who lived in Canada and the northeast. When boys hit puberty, they took them into the wilderness and gave them a drug called 'wysoccan' which is *double* the potency of LSD. After three weeks of taking this drug, they they forgot what it was to be a boy and became a man in doing so. Forgetting the old ways—*that's* what it means to be a man."

His breath smelled like metal and things incombustible. Familiar somehow. I tried moving further from him on the couch but was trapped against the armrest. He reached to grab his Diet Coke, hand missing the mug, feeling the space to the right of it, inching along in the wrong direction. I moved the mug closer to his hand and he fingered the ceramic handle and brought it to his lips before speaking again.

"I'll pay you $100,000 in a lump sum when the job is done. I determine when the job is done. You will provide updates whenever I ask. That's it."

"I will need to verify this arrangement with my superiors before I may proceed."

"You mentioned that already, darling, but this one will be off the record. Do you understand?"

A novel arrangement. My brother used to assign every client to me, but now I just got automated email assignments from Headquarters. The email had the name, address, and request of the client, which was enough for me to go on.

"What is the name of the Creative and what type of memory are you looking to acquire?"

"Her name is Nora Rincón," he said, folding one leg over the other in recline.

"Where can I make her acquaintance?"

"There's a rundown library in Tijuana where she works."

"What is it you are seeking?"

"A place—one that can only be found by searching her memories."

My mind flipped through the different investments I could make with $100,000, the largest sum ever offered to me for one job. I had a dream investment that entailed a start-up that would copyright concepts before they reached the conceptual phase and this funding would be useful. It was my brother's idea.

"How long until I have to decide?"

"You decide now."

Mr. Bray's blindness had the unsettling effect of close attention with no eye contact; what signified inattention in sighted people was the inverse for him. My gaze settled on his harelip that reached toward his nose in a hook shape.

"I will draw up a contract," I said, buttoning my suit coat.

"There is no contract. This is a handshake deal. Understand?"

"With respect, $100,000 is a large sum. How can I know, without a binding contract, that you will release the payment when the job is done?"

"What—you want collateral, darling? That's a reasonable request, let's see…" he said, running a hand over the scruff of his chin. "You see Brutus over there on the wall?"

I craned my neck to look at the 36-inch buffalo head staring at me, its horns curling out from his face to frame his ruffled hair. I nodded, then remembered he couldn't see me.

"Yes."

"That is one of the last buffalo in this country. If you deliver and I fail to come up with the money, take that and sell it. It's worth more than I'm offering."

I looked from the eyes of the buffalo to that of Mr. Bray, neither of which could look back at me. His hand hovered before me.

"Okay," I said, shaking his hand.

If there was some rationale as to why I agreed to this arrangement, why this particular assignment appealed to me, I cannot recall it now. Maybe I agreed just so I could leave.

"We'll be in touch, Sol."

I took the stairs down, nodding to the housekeeper holding the front door open and walked home under the swaying eucalyptus trees, trying to convince myself that something routine had just happened, trying not to think about how he knew my name.

My next trip to Tijuana featured the things I'd come to expect from that place—kids doing handstands on the crosswalk that led to the area where cops protect pimps who protect prostitutes who protect notions of what Tijuana is. While waiting for a car, I watched mechanics take a late lunch, their sweat-stained hats resting on their knees while they ate carne asada tacos and drank Coke from glass bottles. The car pulled to the curb and I got in and said the address of the maquiladora. The car navigated a roundabout to an onramp near the pedestrian crossing. The freeway paralleled the border, both undulating in unison along the hills before it led down the side of a canyon lined with houses overlooking a ravine. The landscape levelled out to a wide street where the freeway ended at the beach community of Playas de Tijuana. At a stoplight, I saw a man sleeping in a hammock strung between two trees in a traffic island that doubled as a park. Little pink flowers floated down from a tree and landed on his chest. I had déjà vu constantly with Tijuanenses, suspecting some, like this man, might be former Creatives, but I was never sure and neither were they or so it seemed.

The car took a left and climbed a hill overlooking Playas de Tijuana. The white buildings spread like shattered teeth below, the marine layer coming toward the beach gradually over a navy blue ocean. The street had veins of grass breaking through the asphalt with houses covered in graffiti or beer ads or some strange fusion of the two on either side. The car finally stopped in a cul-de-sac where the maquiladora stood along its perimeter. The front window's tinting peeled up at the corners; salty air corroded the door handle with orange rust beside a sign that had no words, only a symbol—an hourglass. Half-opened filing cabinets surrounded the cobwebbed reception desk where a blinking phone sat. The ocean-facing lobby windows were covered with X-Acto knife markings. The interior doors opened a few minutes later and Paco walked in, an AK-47 slung across his back, his bald head so smooth and moisturized it reflected the light, which, given that he was a foot shorter than me, was something I never failed to notice. He greeted me and I followed him to the walkway that overlooked the warehouse floor. Cords spewed from the center of the room like leeches, duct-taped to the ground every few feet, connecting everything—generators to computers to hard drives to the routers housing the network on a wheeled cart beside diesel canisters, one of which leaked. The ceiling's A/C vents and the diesel-powered generators gave the room a steady hum. We took the stairs down to the floor, stopping at the first station. A Creative sat unconscious in a wheelchair beside the desk with a Curator filtering through his memories on the computer.

The Curators were competing for some new prize that was this month's incentive from Headquarters. From what I gathered, each row was a team and had a captain and the team with the best turnover rate got a prize. They had masking tape across the backs of each chair with their nicknames written in all caps. The veteran Curators were deciding if the new hire at the end of the row was a deadweight. I turned to the Curator beside me and asked what the prize was that month and her reply was something about an Ensenada cruise. HR must have acquired some comped seats and negotiated the rest at an extreme discount, increasing productivity and profit margin while simultaneously establishing camaraderie and interpersonal communication. I remember the day we set up the cubicles—how proud each Curator was to have his own desk. This row's captain had a framed photo of her son in one corner, and a tiny cactus potted in another beside a certificate commemorating the month where she'd turned over four hundred Creatives. Headquarters encouraged this type of personalization of space because it raised retention by 25 percent.

I looked at the wire that ran from the gel pads adhered to the Creative's head to the desktop computer, where my eyes tracked the cursor absentmindedly, watching as it selected the thumbnail image of a memory. She dragged the thumbnail all the way across the screen, depositing it into the *Transfer* folder and moving on to new memories. Paco and I walked past row after row of Creatives—many of them young men, some of them young women, a few old ones. Curators flipped pages of instructions. Two young boys sat in a wooden pew against the wall with a couple buckets each, taking the gel pads from the first bucket, untangling the wires, and dipping a paintbrush into a canister of adhesive they applied to the pads. After waiting a few seconds, they put a little square of paper over each pad then tossed them in the second bucket. A third boy in a Power Rangers shirt and lace-less shoes slept under the pew. The boy on the left looked around to see if anyone was watching before he put his little nose over the nitrocellulose and inhaled until he fell back in a haze, giving the canister to the second boy who did the same.

I watched one Creative awake from submersion and try to wrench her arms from the Velcro straps, her sandals tapping the ground in an anxious dance. The Curator removed the gel pads from her head, and freed her from the straps of the wheelchair, then escorted her to the Pay Distribution Center which was merely a repurposed ATM. The Creative looked at the number written in Sharpie on the back of her hand, then pressed the keypad. A few moments passed and the machine played a jingle before releasing a crisp manila envelope filled with the allotted amount of bills. The old woman opened the envelope and counted, mouthing the sum before turning to the Curator and spewing curses. The Curator pointed at me and she hobbled over and recited her grievance. I recognized her as Uno, the old woman whose nickname came from being the first documented Creative in this maquiladora—her ID number: 0001. She returned every month escorted by the same young man with long brown hair, and each month she parted with more and more intimate memories—as if gradually extending the radius of what to let go. She had one blue eye and one brown eye—a condition called heterochromia iridis—like two people trapped in one face.

"No hablo español," I said.

She repeated herself, saying it louder, but I repeated my answer which was Standard Operating Procedure in these situations. Paco sidled up beside me. The old woman was brimming with tears as she registered the AK-47 strapped on Paco's shoulder. She hobbled away with that day's payment as new Creatives filed in through the corrugated metal door that rolled up and flooded the back entrance with light. The Recruiter directed them to the empty wheelchairs beside Curators busy checking their Facebooks or clipping their nails or reapplying Chapstick in the time between sessions.

Paco pointed to his watch and we walked outside and closed the roll-up door behind us, then collapsed into lawn chairs that looked out over Playas de Tijuana. I usually would not partake in social interludes like this, but it was a good opportunity to stay abreast of advantageous information. With Paco, you had to separate fact from rumor, which was often unstraightforward. For example, one time Paco told me that we'd beta-tested a new product line with local prisons in the U.S. to search inmates' memories for evidence of committed crimes. Even after promising returns—according to Paco—the product was discontinued. So I always partook in this afternoon ritual, ready for information.

I handed Paco the binoculars and he looked for whales. He shook his head and gave them back and I put them in the pocket of the chair as he uncapped a Modelo from the cooler and handed it to me so I could carefully unwrap the golden foil around the edge. We watched workers lay track at the construction site that stretched north all the way to the border, a large dust cloud drifting off toward the beach.

"Who seen weirder shit you or me?" Paco said.

I thought for a few moments then searched the construction site to find something to comment on and recalibrate the conversation—not because I was unwilling to answer his question, but because it would start a futile game of one-upmanship.

"You, I'd imagine."

"Try me, boss, c'mon. What you got?"

So commenced the one-upping. I considered whether the most efficient means of ending the discussion would entail offering a meager example and allowing him to trounce it, or to offer the most bizarre example in the hopes it would not be topped.

"I don't know."

"Yes you do, c'mon boss."

He was clearly unyielding, so I enacted strategy number one, offering the meager example in the hopes he would easily outmatch it and end the inquiry.

"I saw a researcher pay $1,500 for memories of living in the Tijuana dump."

"Weak sauce."

"I guess you win, then."

"What else?"

Another tactical mistake—I was playing into his hands.

"A retired colonel paid $2,800 for memories of menopause."

He shook his head as he scraped a dirt clod off the AK-47's barrel that leaned against his lawn chair. "You can do better, boss. I mean I know this nun who paid three grand for a memory of anal. Come on."

I closed my eyes and pretended to think hard—scrunching my

face—even though I had the answer to his question from the outset.

"Alright," I said, opening my eyes. "There was this accountant who paid $4,500 for the memories of an amputation."

"Of what?"

"A hand."

"That's nothing. I seen beheadings," Paco said.

"Memories of beheadings don't exist."

"I know," he said. "Hey boss, we should get limes for these."

He drank the last of his beer and threw it down the hill and we watched it roll for several seconds until it broke against a rock. Sometimes, on a clear day with no marine layer, we could see the barren Coronado Islands off the coast. Paco always said he'd sail out to one, but he didn't know how to sail or anyone who did and never bothered to elaborate.

We went back inside and passed a ten-year-old Creative at a station—straps bunched around her shoulders because they were too big to hold her little arms in place, the Curator scanning her memories at the desk beside her. Paco got the attention of this Curator and made a circle motion with his finger, signaling to wrap things up. This message passed down that row and the next and the next, until every Curator was unhooking external hard drives with that day's memories and depositing them in a plastic bucket in the center of the room, then filing back to their cubicles to pick up their things, zipping jackets, locking drawers, shutting down computers. After the last Curator had left, Paco grabbed the bucket by one of the handles and I took the other and we walked it up the metal stairs to the top level.

"You ever wonder why we use such old tech?" Paco said as we rested on the landing and looked out at the morass of cords, wheelchairs, generators, laptops—equipment from the past.

"Headquarters informed me it's a precautionary measure."

"What's that mean?"

"I don't know."

"I bet it keeps everything hardwired, ya know, not able to be hacked. What's the word?"

"Analog."

We walked to the car, opened the door, and set the memories on the seat and I got in. Paco lit a cigarette and smoked on the curb. I moved to close the door but Paco put his hand on it.

"Listen, boss, I hear your brother died. I'm sorry about that."

I nodded as his hand released and I closed the door. The car pulled away and wove through the streets that ran between houses huddled as if for warmth before stopping at the end of the border queue. The sky grew darker, the sun's exit leaving the horizon pink. Churros from a handful of vendors with pushcarts saturated the air. A twelve-year-old drank clear liquid then flicked a lighter near his mouth, spitting a plume of fire that made the tourists shed pesos. The sombreros and blankets and plastic Jesuses and ceramic Virgins and knit bags sat beside cartel memorabilia of bullet-ridden license plates and soldering irons apparently used in interrogations.

A woman guided her mentally disabled granddaughter between the cars. She had fashioned a little sign that hung from the child's neck on which was written something in Spanish I assume provided an explanation in the form of a plea. Hands emerged from windows and deposited crumpled bills into the plastic cup the cross-eyed girl held and when they passed me, I made eye contact with the woman, whose gaze I can only describe as cast-iron. Near the front of the line, a man sat on a concrete divider, his shirt pulled above his stomach which was swollen to the size of a watermelon. He rubbed the scars that coated his stomach like lipstick stains. By the streetlamp's light, I watched his eyes tilt on a level axis at each car and only flicker alive when a hand emerged from a window to transfer cash without touching him. It wasn't until I saw the tattoo of his forearm that I recognized him as one of our first wave of Creatives. His hair was longer now. He kept his cash in a t-shirt pocket he covered with the hand that wasn't scratching the stomach wounds. I watched him nod off and wake up a few times before two young men approached him, one of them spooning something out of a bag to feed him while the other counted the pocket money.

After crossing, the car merged onto the 5-North and I watched the southbound cars' orange eyes search the pavement while signs for National City and Downtown passed overhead. I picked up one of the hard drives and felt its scuffed edges and thought about my brother. He died fifty-two days ago. The final time I saw him, he said his next client would be his last. I understand now what he meant.

CHAPTER 2

I couldn't sleep, so I walked around Balboa Park because I could see time measured via the security guard shift changes, the sprinklers turning on, the mockingbirds' wakening—every cycle assuring me the evening was uneternal. Amid each of these routines would usually be an anomaly, like the apparitional coyote that appeared, its snout bouncing above the damp grass and onto the lawn-bowling field where it stopped and lay, head nestled in its autumnal fur, large ears bending to the sounds of the night. I crossed the bridge astride the road's double-yellow line, reaching the bell tower that glowed neon pink from hidden lights. Balboa Park was built to recall an era that never existed here, with its nostalgic Spanish Colonial buildings and museums between lawns and chaparral vegetation and non-native trees planted so long ago they felt indigenous. When they built it, Balboa must've felt like a spectacle. Now it just felt like San Diego.

The park was quiet except for the crickets and the occasional car. Avoiding the homeless was a territorial dance, the mutual trust measured in the amount of feet they kept between you and them. I stopped at the pond where the ducks slept on the grass, balancing on one foot with their heads buried in their wings looking like a teed-up football. Rabbits jumped among the bushes near the free museum that held a Rembrandt. People slept in the hallway alcoves, or on the threshold of museum doors or the stage of the amphitheater that hosted the LA Philharmonic earlier that week. I took the footbridge to the cactus gardens but turned back when I heard humping in a tent that overlooked the canyon. The bus stopped on Park Boulevard and a man wearing a gas mask and a Stetson got off and started up the ramp of the footbridge. I followed as he passed the fountain, taking each stride as if fated. He arrived at the Japanese Friendship Garden entrance, scaled the small fence and descended into the gully. I looked into the darkness for several minutes from a deck, seeing nothing, then—as I made to leave—a small flame glimmered. I watched until the light disappeared.

A car collected me from the stoplight near the dog park after enough time had passed and took me to the nearest Denny's where the waitress recognized me but never said my name because I never mentioned it. She merely nodded to me and poured coffee into a mug that always had an unfunny saying on it like "Keep Calm and COFFEE." Fifteen minutes later, two eggs and hash browns were set before me. I did not even like eggs and hash browns, but the first time I came here, the night after my brother died, she asked me what I would like to eat—even though my plan was just to order coffee—and I pointed to the first thing I saw on the menu and that is what she brought. I did that each week until she just started asking "The usual?" and I would nod and thank her then half-eat the food.

A table of regulars—former truckers who had never retrained and survived off unemployment, part-time fishing, and disability checks—sat beside me. Their waitress called them "Lovey" as she touched their shoulders and asked if they were doing alright and by "alright" she meant in terms of refills, silverware, and condiments. Across from the truckers were two widowers who ordered iced tea and omelets and talked about hunting and what they missed about their wives.

Instead of allocating funding toward caulking that does not

spill over the glass panes or refurbishing the linoleum tabletops to address the scratches, Denny's offered endless pancakes and bottomless coffee for five dollars, creating a purgatorial comfort festooned with lava lampshades, red pleather booths and windows with Venetian blinds that were never drawn. Everything was stackable—the plates, platters, to-go boxes, dip holders, lids. The laminated menus, vinyl wood floor, and glass salt/pepper shakers made it so a massacre could occur and the place could reopen an hour later after a good hose-down.

I watched the customers and staff circulate—the waitress with a sparkly bow in her hair, the high schooler who changed the music, the aging busboy who wore a rubber apron. He set a plastic bin on the table adjacent to mine and deposited dirty plates, his fingers catching a dollop of mayonnaise which he wiped on a dish towel slung over his shoulder. The sparkly-bowed waitress asked him to take out the trash and he nodded and gave a puff-cheeked sigh—his only form of protest. When he came to my table and said "Done?" I wondered if he recognized me at all or if he never looked long enough to notice who were regulars and who were not. I have spent entire nights watching his wrinkled elbows that look like fish mouths, wondering whether anyone was waiting for him when he put his keys on the kitchen counter. Wondering if there were any Save-The-Dates on his fridge.

As I watched him clear the plates from a table under the lamplight, something welled up in me. Not pity, but envy. It took me a while to realize I was jealous of him, jealous of his capacity to work the graveyard shift at Denny's night after night after night.

When he got off at 4 a.m. he sat in his car for five minutes—eyes closed, hands on the steering wheel—listening to a meditative voice through his stereo that wasn't loud enough to be heard from the bushes. I wished that when he said "Done?" I invited him over for dinner, where he could confirm or recalibrate my narratives about him while enjoying my balcony that overlooked the city and a bottle of wine that cost more than his car payment. He could tell me about the women he regretted not asking out and about life before the internet. I wished I could offer to pay his rent in exchange for telling me what he listened to those five minutes in the car and if it worked. But I don't.

I left Denny's, taking a car that dropped me at Spruce Street near the footbridge known for couples etching their names on padlocks and securing them to the bridge's webbed railing to signify their love's indestructability; among them, was one bearing my brother's name, Jordan, alongside his ex-girlfriend's. When his fiancée learned about the padlock years later, she demanded he remove it—giving him bolt cutters for Christmas—which he refused on principle. Over Christmas dinner, Jordan articulated how the padlock was meaningless because the love it signified was nonexistent, launching into a condescending explanation of semiotic theory which could've been elided by saying simply that removing the padlock would validate its meaning, while his fiancée argued leaving it validated its meaning. They broke up the following day.

Eventually the matter resolved itself—the city determined the bridge unsafe due to the destabilizing weight of thousands of padlocks that'd accumulated over the years and removed all of them. I never asked my brother about this broken engagement during the few times a year we spoke. Instead, he would tell me about biking these streets at night, preferring the efficiency of biking to alternative forms of exercise because of its speed and maneuverability. I pictured him passing the places I did now, like the sports bar where men guzzled IPA's before going back to wives they'd cheat on if they were organized enough, or the French restaurant where staff bickered with retirees playing chess at its outdoor tables, resolute to finish before the lights went out. He probably turned around when the boarded-up boutiques started lining the streets beside the gay bars and night clubs and homeless corners. I continued past these places because of the inertia of my routine, which deposited me in a hospital's waiting room at the end of the street.

I sat in the corner of the waiting room where parents were praying, hoping God would tip the scales. The labored breathing of a man beside me sounded like he had three noses and no mouth. A five-year-old made a bed of three chairs and his shoes ignited with blue lights when he kicked in his sleep. A Filipino family waited on news—a few of the boys joking around on their phones while the matriarch wrung a magazine in her plump little hands.

A doctor came out to tell the praying parents—*your daughter/not responding/I'm sorry*—which made the father collapse against a vending machine. The doctor delegated and moved on. The kid slept another hour on the chairs until a woman in blue scrubs emerged from the double doors, her shoes squeaking on the disinfected hallway. She knelt, scooped the boy up, and left. Two nurses returned from a smoke break, comparing theories about a scandal that involved a doctor and a patient.

A grandfatherly man walked in, sat beside me, and took out the contents of his breakfast from a paper sack: apple, chocolate milk, gas station tamale, flavored peanuts. The straw fell from the chocolate milk, so I picked it up and handed it to him.

"Thanks," he said, peeling off the plastic and stabbing the straw through the top of the milk. He unfurled a map where tiny holes had formed along the edges of each fold, then unpocketed a pen and removed the cap with his teeth, spitting it out to sip the rest of his chocolate milk. Red circles and Xs dotted the map. A bit of chewed apple landed on North Park.

"My daughter's a nurse in San Diego. She works at a hospital, but I don't know which one, so I been goin' around, waiting and waiting and waiting for the nurses to change shifts so I can find her. This is the fourteenth one I've come to."

He'd crossed out most of those along the bay. I saw one he missed in University Heights but did not mention it as his eyes implored the map, darting from one circle to the next before looking at me.

"She needs to know I'm back and won't leave again."

Nurses came and went—filing paperwork, getting coffee, calling patients—and each time the hallway door opened he sprung up then sank back, hands on armrests, bottom ascending and descending hydraulically. He opened a tamale, the steam wafting around his face as he considered his next destination. I got up and left—exiting into those blue-gray hours when we're all equally confused.

I ordered coffee from a machine on Sixth Avenue just for the warmth of the cup in my hands. The coyote had left an oval indentation on the bowling green that disturbed several old men in white uniforms as I strolled back across the bridge that extends over the 163 freeway. The lampposts clicked off one at a time, ceding to the natural light. The homeless folded their bedding as museum staff folded brochures, each at their respective locations and each pausing only to rub their eyes.

I drank my coffee while sitting on the rim of the fountain that held coins made shiny by the chlorine. The water began to swirl, humming, as if animated by wishes trying to escape. Insomniacs carry a secret because every person we meet assumes we slept somewhere between the hours of 10 p.m. and 8 a.m. and we maintain this assumption by being fully coherent, not disheveled or bloodshot or sweaty, which requires a special practice. All these extra hours develop a heightened awareness that can evaluate every situation from every angle, which is why when I first met Mr. Bray, his request did not intimidate me. Life is only opaque due to the constraint of time—one that does not apply to me. I can see everything if I devote enough attention to it. Everything remains under control because I see every possible outcome. Or so I believed at the time.

CHAPTER 3

The sole purpose of my next trip to Tijuana was to find Nora Rincón—the young woman who had a memory my client, Mr. Bray, required. The only information I had to go on was that she worked at a library. A quick search of Tijuana libraries showed several options. I created a new email account and signed up for the newsletters of each, receiving dozens of automated responses, one of which was signed Nora Rincón. I drafted an email to the address listed on the "Contact Us" page of their website, mentioning that I would like to become a patron of the arts in Tijuana, starting with a contribution to that library, hoping Nora would be the person receiving these emails. For credibility purposes, I imitated the tone of global corporations' philanthropic arms, mentioning my intention to uplift the youth of Tijuana through the renovation of a public reading space. I received a response an hour later from Nora, inviting me to meet her at the library to discuss this opportunity further.

The following day at 4:00 p.m., I stood in front of the library looking for a trashcan to deposit the lime-green flyers for discounted drinks thrust toward me down the gauntlet of tourist bars that littered the route there. There were none to be found, only sticker-covered skateboard racks and a drinking fountain with spouts at human and dog heights.

"Sol?" I looked up to see a young woman coming around the corner holding two coffee cups. "Okay, listen very carefully. I'm going in first then you will follow me fifteen seconds later with the coffee. Remember that—*fifteen seconds*. Carlos, the librarian, is very strict about not allowing drinks so I always have to sneak this shit in. What I'll do is distract Carlos by asking him about his love life, then you will slip behind me on my left—remember that, *ON MY LEFT*—with the coffees concealed under your little sweater vest thing you're wearing. Got it?"

I nodded. She handed me the coffees.

"Okay—*showtime*."

She disappeared inside the library doors and I counted to fifteen and lifted the hem of my sweater vest over the coffees, then opened the door and hunch-walked through the metal detector past Nora as she talked to a bald gentleman arranging returns on a cart, his steroidal chest tapering off into a small torso and skinny ankles. I shuffled to a table near the left side of the library in a manner as casual as possible given the coffee concealment. Nora joined me a minute later. She felt the weight of the first cup, then the second cup, then the first one again, brow furrowing. She opened the lid and froze, staring at the foamy top of her latte. Her latte had a powdered-chocolate dusting in the shape of a flag. I realized her paralysis would remain unless I intervened.

"Is there some concern?"

"Ramón didn't use the eagle-snake-cactus stencil. He just eyeballed it, making the Mexican flag look like the Italian flag."

The milky bubbles hollowed out in the middle, thinning and dissipating into the espresso underneath, making the chocolate powder condense and streak. Nora shook her head and drank while I prepared for the tell-me-about-yourself-ing. Instead, she launched into talking about the library.

"So, this fine establishment was built fifty years ago after members of the community got fed up waiting for a half-decent public library within walking distance. Funding was scrounged together from the odd grant here and there, donations, allocations from the state, etc., etc. Fast forward to today—yours truly calls the shots of where the money goes, and boy oh boy do we need some of that good kush."

"I'm sorry?"

"Clams."

"I don't understand."

"Fetti."

She could tell that I still did not understand, so she finally explained, saying each word slowly as if teaching the alphabet.

"Fetti—F-E-T-T-I—fettucine—cheese—cheddar—MONEY."

"I see."

"Someone's gotta keep the lights on." Just then, the fluorescent trac lighting above flickered and she pointed up at it without breaking eye contact.

"Speaking of cheese, see Carlos over there?" Nora nodded toward the librarian at the front desk. "He's an ex-con. They got him for mauling his ex's new boyfriend with a cheese grater. While in prison, he learned the Dewey Decimal System and became the librarian here when he was released."

"How did you come to work here?"

Follow-up questions such as these were always effective because it kept the conversationalist talking while also appearing to build rapport with me as I mapped the conversational terrain where I wanted it to go.

"When he was on parole, he caught me kicking over all the trashcans in celebration after landing my first kickflip outside. I remember him snatching my board and telling me the only way I'd get it back is if I helped him at the library. That was two years ago."

I looked around the room and realized I could walk the perimeter of the library in 90 seconds. Like the rest of Tijuana, every square foot of space was used in some way. Getting to the watercooler meant navigating through an obstacle course of book towers and random chairs either piled with binders or old paperbacks needing a home. Multicolored bean bag chairs were stacked in the kids' corner. All the tables were plastic and collapsible. I watched an old man in the Histórico section feel the binding of every book on the shelf before settling on one with a canvas cover, thumbing through it and putting it back, armpit stains peek-a-booing with each motion, until eventually settling on a thin copy with a green cover.

I tilted my head to see the book resting under Nora's elbow. She noticed me doing this and held it up so I could see *Patti McGee: A Biography*.

"Who is this?"

"Patti McGee? No? Can anyone help me out here?" she said, looking around as if for support. "You don't know who *Patti McGee* is?"

She leaned out of her seat nearly sideways to ensure the librarian couldn't see her drinking a beverage in a non-beverage area.

"Ah, the female skateboarder. Of course," I said, after googling.

She looked at me with the condescending pity of a physician toward an anti-vaxxer.

"Patti McGee isn't just a female skateboarder, she's the *first* professional lady skater *ever*. At nineteen. Nineteen! She was from San Diego. Without her, there's no Tony Hawk."

"Oh, okay."

"That's all you have to say? This woman practically invents a new sport and a new industry, travels the country in the 60s kicking ass in skate competitions, gets on the cover of LIFE Magazine, goes on national TV in front of millions of people and teaches all those motherfuckers how to skate *barefoot* and all you have to say is *Huh, okay*?"

"I mean, that's impressive."

"Goddamn, dude. What've *you* done?"

Nora hid her coffee as the reformed cheese graterer returned books to their corresponding shelves and went back to the front desk. The skylight showed the clouds moving. Two kids opened the door to a room flooded by blue light as their mother relaxed with a romance novel at the table under the noticeboard holding flyers for community gardens and skate competitions and a list of free days at local museums.

"That's a little movie theater." Nora said, nodding toward the blue-lit room. "It has a ton of movies to choose from, all dubbed in Spanish. More lettuce would mean we could afford better versions. It's pretty rough going right now."

"Tell me more about that."

I remembered this line from a client who was a therapist and often forgot to codeswitch.

"The dubbed lines don't really match the actor's mouths all that well, but if we had the money, we could pay for a better subscription and get the quality editions. Most of the movies are pretty old but there's some good stuff in there."

"What is your favorite movie?"

She shrugged and said, "I don't know the *names* of the movies I just like to get drunk and pick one randomly."

My attention drifted to the mother reading her romance novel, her eyebrows bouncing as she read one of the lines. Beside her, a teenager sharpened a pencil and let the filings fall like orange peels onto her textbook, spinning the pencil round and round as if hoping to ward off her exam date with each spiral. Two tables from her, a man with neck tattoos read a Japanese cookbook, turning the pages with reverence to ensure they did not crinkle in his fingertips.

"Name me a single better place to put your money than this one," she said, as a group of kids tumbled across the carpet. They crawled, trenchlike, to the children's section and picked out hardbacks bigger than their faces, grabbing them from each other before they could even read the pages. One of them realized his chair made a flatulating sound, which made them giggle until Carlos got up from the front desk, his musculature nearly bursting through his shirt. They cowered before him as he snatched a Dr. Seuss book from a kid's trembling hands and said something in Spanish that made their fear invert to glee that was shushed as he started reading in various high-pitched voices—a 250-pound man with licorice veins doing the voice of the Lorax. Nora smiled, the first one I'd seen from her.

"So what's your deal, you don't have any friends?" she said.

"I'm sorry?"

"Are you, like, desperately in need of a friend or something? You came here saying you wanted to be 'a patron of the arts in Tijuana,' but you seem not to care about *anything* I've been telling you. You haven't even asked for a tour of the premises or anything like that. It's a bit mystifying. What are you *really* doing here?"

She narrowed her eyes and leaned forward, having to peer up to meet my eyeline. I considered that she could sense an ulterior motive, but this seemed unlikely, so I substantiated my original reason with a more believable premise.

"To be honest, I will get a significant tax write-off for this contribution, so that relates to part of my motivation, but I am also interested in the service this library offers."

"You think you can just pop down for a day, drop a grip of cash, and leave?"

She collected her dark hair into a ball and knotted it into a bun with a hair tie.

"No. Actually, I would like to spend time getting to know the library."

She leaned back, weighing something in her mind. The perforated ceiling tiles above us had gaps every fourth or fifth, exposing the steel wire. The lights shone yellow like egg yolk over the oatmeal carpet and broken fire alarms. Her gaze drifted toward the framed skateboarding awards on the wall. She picked up her book and stood.

"I gotta take off. Let's meet up again and talk specifics. I got some projects that could use your support. When are you back down?"

I made a show of checking my calendar, swiping up theatrically at my phone.

"How is next Thursday?" I said.

"Thursday's fine but it'll have to be at my brother's softball game. Bring a seat cushion or your ass'll get sore. I'll email you the info." She looked over my shoulder and saw Carlos at the front desk, his back to us. "I can't be seen with this, here, take it."

She slid the empty cup across the table then sauntered over to Carlos by the metal detectors. I saw his head bobbing with the ripples of conversation as Nora pointed to me, then left through the double doors as he got up, marched over, and grabbed the cups before I could offer an explanation while Nora watched from the door and laughed.

⧗

```
CREATIVE: [0000] <DAVID BRAY>
TRANSCRIPT BY: [JORDAN ANDREWS]
*DIALOGUE APPROXIMATED - TRANSLATED FROM SPANISH*

START .......................................
We are in a room high up in a building
potentially in the central business district. She
stubs a cigarette out on an ashtray. The drapes
```

move with the breeze. She blows smoke toward the corner of the room. I tell her to stop and she does.

"Do you know the name for having one blue eye and one brown eye?" I ask her.

I caress her shoulder and her feedback is positive.

"No."

"It's called heterochromia iridis."

"I don't like it."

"Why?"

"Kids used to tease me. Called me 'ojos malos'."

"They should envy you, darling."

"Why?"

"Because every person you meet will never forget you. All those brats will still remember you long after you have forgotten them."

Her expression changes. She shifts away from me in the bed.

"We don't need to talk," she said. "I just didn't want to be alone."

"Why?"

"I'm scared."

"Of what?"

She turned back toward me, the lamplight fell on half her face.

"I went to a funeral today. At the ceremony … I don't know how to explain it."

"Explain what?"

"The miracle."

"What do you mean?"

"You won't believe me."

"I will. Tell me."

"A blind woman saw today. She hadn't been able to see in thirty years but her eyes opened today and she still sees. In one moment. She could not see and then she could. A man in a wheelchair prayed over her and then she saw. This is just one of many miracles that have happened there."

"Where?"

She turned back over in the bed, away from me.

"Where?"

"Where the orphans are buried."

END ....

CHAPTER 4

Cars dropped off the softball players under a sky of monochrome blue. They spread out on each side of the field, taking their time stretching as middle-aged men do. The infield was mostly dirt with patches of grass. A park ranger truck sidled up to me and Nora got out with a man I assumed was her brother. He paused at the car door he'd just locked and pulled the handle several times then circled around to the passenger door and pulled that handle the same number of times then clicked the key fob twice and, finally, turned to us.

"Gabe, this is—" she paused. "What's your name again?"

"Sol."

"This is Sol. He's come to offer *a shit ton* of money to support the library."

"Good to meet you, Sol," Gabe said, shaking my hand. He was the type of person whose resting face is a smile, one that left creases on his forehead. "Well, I'm gonna go warm up," he said, his voice carrying a lisp that endeared you to him for some reason unknown. He went to the field, athletic shorts hanging just past his knees, bat and glove in tow.

Nora and I climbed up the bleachers. She placed a dog-eared book beside her on the stainless-steel bench then flipped through a binder to a blank scorecard, uncapped a pen, and wrote down each player she saw on the field. Gabe's team, as well as Nora, wore white jerseys with red sleeves that ran halfway down like capris for the arms. Gabe did several stretches—across the chest, over the head, waving windmill-like—then joined a teammate in a preparatory "warm-up" that entailed throwing the ball back and forth, his partner gradually increasing the distance to make each toss longer. Afterward, he took to the mound to practice his parabolic slow pitch, each one thudding near the plate. Nora opened a bag of sunflower seeds, nodded to me, then started pouring them all over the seat until I intervened, cupping both hands to catch the stream until they overflowed at which point she poured herself some.

"So, is this the first regional, Southern California, middle-aged, civil servant, softball game you've been to?" she said, tucking her knees under her softball jersey so only her red Converse poked out.

I nodded.

"The Ocean Sidewinders—those bitches over there—came down from Oceanside for this. They drew a decent crowd considering the drive."

"Do you come to every game?"

"Of course I do, who else'd heckle JFK?"

"Who?"

"Joe *Fucking* Kline—their best hitter. He's in the three-hole."

After a couple groundouts a beefy, neckless man stepped up to the plate. His jersey had frayed edges where sleeves should be. He blew a kiss to Gabe, who was pitching, and pointed his bat toward the fence. The Ocean Sidewinders cheered. Gabe looked to Nora from the mound and shook his head and Nora shook hers. Just as Gabe let go of the ball, she shouted *EAT SHIT JOE KLINE!* and the batter whiffed and collected himself, trying not to acknowledge her. Another pitch came along with another request for Joe Kline to consume excrement as he swung and missed. Their crowd booed Nora, who puffed up like a Grizzly.

"I'd appreciate it if you could be *quiet,*" Joe Kline said, stepping out of the box to point his bat at her. "I'm going deep off your brother. I'll wave to you as I round third base."

"Well, I'm going deep on your father—and *I'll* wave to *you* as I round *his* third base."

"My father is *paralyzed.*"

"Hasn't stopped me before!"

He stepped back into the box, fuming, then struck out and threw his bat against the chain-link fence.

"This is porn for me," Nora said, grabbing a handful of sunflower seeds and watching as Joe Kline threw every piece of equipment he could get his hands on. The teams swapped field for dugout and Gabe stepped into the batter's box while the moon hovered over the field like a third floodlight. Gabe wore batting gloves and detached then reattached the Velcro four times on each hand. He twisted his torso three times one way and three times the other then touched every corner of the box with his bat and looked toward the pitcher. Nora smiled.

"My brother has OCD. His routines can be fun to watch if I'm in the mood."

The pitcher performed an exaggerated wind-up then lobbed the ball toward the plate and Gabe made contact and hustled toward first base—his stubby legs accelerating faster than expected—and made it safe. The next batter doubled and Gabe ran to third base, then to home plate on what Nora called a "sac fly." Soon, Gabe's team was back on the pitching side. Nora zeroed-in on the first batter.

"Oh *shit*. Gonzo's up. Dude fucking CRUSHES. And he isn't fazed by heckling—believe me, *I've tried*. I haven't shown him any skin yet, but it just might come to that if he keeps his OPS in the 900's." Nora said. "This is not gonna end well, shit shit shit."

One swing and the ball coasted over the fence, clearing it by twenty feet, while Gonzo trotted around the bases like a gentleman.

"I know how this whole charade must look to you."

"Can you please clarify?"

"My investment in this middle-aged civil servant league." She glanced over. "Do you have any siblings?"

"No."

I only said this because going into the details of my brother and what happened would divulge too much too soon. To answer "yes" would lead to an unnecessary amount of evasion and lies while answering a simple "no" was easier in every way.

"The truth is I don't care about softball in the least. I do, however, care about what my brother cares about and—for whatever reason—he cares a lot about this weekly softball game. So it's my job to set him up for success." She looked at me, checking for comprehension, but something in my face underwhelmed her. "Never mind. If you don't know, you don't know."

"What is it I don't know?"

"That you should be all-in on supporting what family you're lucky to have."

Nora stood up and gathered her dark hair together, tying it in a bun as the teams exchanged places again. The sunflower seeds made my tongue a tarmac of salt and BBQ spice. Over a few years of building rapport with clients, I had learned to tolerate a wide array of behaviors. I pretended to love cognac. Lost $10,000 dollars on bets at the Del Mar racetrack. Toured the USS Midway and feigned astonishment at the vintage planes housed there. This was a new frontier.

"Speaking of family ... you seem like an art history aficionado, are you familiar with the Medicis?"

"No." Of course I was.

"The Medicis were a merchant family in Italy in the 1300s or 1800s or whatever and they used all of that wealth and power to be patrons for the arts. Cool, right? They commissioned work from Raphael and Michelangelo—all the turtles. Now, what if I told you that you could partake in this long, rich tradition? You're Italian right?"

The House of Medici essentially ruled Italy for five hundred years controlling, at certain points, the papacy, the monarchy, the market, the music, and the art in Italy. Post-Renaissance Europe had never experienced such a sprawling and influential organization and nothing like it would be replicated. A dilapidated library in Tijuana was a bit different.

"Sounds interesting."

"I'll say! And guess what—those dudes shelled out *a lot* to make it happen." She closed her binder, her gaze returning to me after a few seconds. "So the question remains—how much do you really care?"

"The ceiling of my contribution would be twenty thousand dollars."

She looked me up and down.

"Dude, your *shoes* nearly cost that." They did not. "Come on, that's not very much money to you, is it? Let's go a bit higher, come on, it's for the kids. Forty grand to start."

"I could possibly manage twenty-two thousand." This felt reasonable given I'd likely be reimbursed for most of it and the rest I could write-off.

"Come on Mr. Medici, level with me. You could *easily* double that, probably triple."

"I could not, unfortunately." I could.

"Okay, okay, 35 G."

"I could—perhaps—do 23, but that would be my ceiling."

"23? The ceiling? For a fella like you?"

She was playing both good-cop and bad-cop, and I am unsure if she knew how strange it came across. She stared, unblinking, at me for more seconds than anyone has ever stared at me unblinking.

"I suppose I could shift certain funds and—depending on the timing—make a contribution of $25,000."

"Are you gonna be eating out of cans for the next month if you do? Level with me dude—30."

She kept saying just the numeral and not adding "thousand" afterward as if to euphemize the magnitude. I performatively weighed the number in my head, miming consideration.

"$26,000—but it will come with a condition."

"28 and you get your condition."

"27 and the condition is that you show me how my contribution will improve the library. I would like to see how you put it to use."

"You mean I just show you how we spend the money?"

I nodded.

She spit on her hand and held it out. "27,000 *BIG ONES*."

I stared, unblinking, at her hand.

"Now you spit on your hand and shake mine and then we have a deal you can't break."

"I don't understand."

"It's in all the old movies. Just do it."

Nora did not lower her hand until I had managed a dime-sized drop of saliva on my own hand and held it out and she took it in hers and squeezed harder than necessary. We heard the ping of a softball bat and her eyes returned to the field in time to see the ball bouncing in a gap between two outfielders. Nora examined the batters up next and flipped to the pages near the front of the binder to check the old, heavily annotated scorecards. I watched the other softball field across from us where kids were ollieing their scooters over bases and smoking. Gabe got to bat once more with a runner on third base, down one run. The pitch came and he swung—hitting the ball all the way to the wall where it was caught, ending the game. A few minutes later, Gabe walked slump-shouldered out to his truck while his teammates talked about where they'd go for drinks. He started a cool-down stretch, his hands flat against the truck's door, calves extended.

"Want to join us for drinks, Sol?"

"Okay." I said, checking Nora for disaffirmation but receiving no sign. "Thank you."

Nora climbed into the truck bed, leaning her head against the back window, and I took the passenger seat beside Gabe. He played Christian music on the stereo and relaxed his arm out the window. Nora did not seem to mind her hair flying everywhere as we coasted down Morena Boulevard, passing laundromats and carpet stores and salons and insurance places you never saw anyone enter or exit—buildings that look like how doing taxes feels. We pulled into the parking lot and walked over to a bar called *The Cantina*. It was thematically constipated—a tiki hut crossed with a Mexican villa. Palm fronds were stapled to the bar and mariachis played in the corner. You could see all the different shops of Old Town from where I sat—the saloon and bank, painted a stately white, with large porches and a covered wagon between them—evoking an Old West that never existed. Gabe ordered a ginger beer for himself and two Coronas for us and we toasted to the Flamethrowers before he left to mingle with his teammates. We watched a drunk woman with a bachelorette sash try to drink from the silverware container she thought was her glass.

"I'm surprised Gabe invited you along, he doesn't usually do that with people he doesn't know," Nora said, wheeling around in her seat to watch a priest walk down the footpath with his old bloodhound that lagged so far behind that the priest paused every tenth step because the leash ran out of slack. The mariachis exited *The Cantina* in favor of an upscale Mexican restaurant across the street that had Diego Rivera prints on the walls, promptly serenading an old woman who smiled and made little fists of delight.

"He feels sorry for you," Nora said, snapping her fingers. "That accounts for the invitation. That motherfucker never saw a stray he didn't like."

As Nora drank her beer, she made predictions on how long each couple we saw on a date would last: "50 years … one night … one night … two nights … life … divorced next year." She set her beer down and looked at me. "So how'd you hear about my library?"

"Google."

"You googled 'libraries that need 30 grand' and mine happened to come up?"

"Yes."

"Hm." She sized up a new couple that'd just sat down at an outdoor table under a heater. "Probably … eighteen months then he cheats on her then—wait, no, I take that back. Eighteen months and she breaks it off, but not because of cheating. She just realizes she doesn't love him. It started as just a little feeling in the back of her head that she dismissed at first, but, over time, slowly grew into a truth that is as solid as anything she's ever known. Once this occurs to her, eighteen months from now, it will feel obvious, like how could she not of known from that very first date in Old Town at that restaurant." She spun toward the bar, reorienting the same intensity of attention toward me. "So, what job do you have that pays you so much and how do I get it?"

I took a moment to filter through my usual answers.

"I'm a Memory Curator."

She rolled her eyes. "We get it, dude, you could've just said 'It's too complicated to explain' and I would've believed you."

Gabe returned with chips and salsa in a green basket.

"So how'd I do out there tonight?" Gabe asked Nora, his lateral lisp inflecting the S.

"Mas o menos."

"I got a hit."

"Yeah in five at-bats. Another performance like that and your batting average will drop below .250. You know who else's batting average is below .250?"

"Who?"

"Dexter Riddlesworth. You really want to be in the same sentence as him?"

Gabe shook his head.

"That's what I thought."

"Tell me what I need to do."

"Practice your hitting."

"How?"

Nora looked at me. "Make this guy pitch to you."

"You think?" Gabe said, the two of them talking as if I weren't there.

"For sure. I just got him to donate 30 grand to the library."

"I believe we settled on—"

"Let's not get into the weeds of it."

We watched kids play hide-and-seek around the giant pepper tree. From our angle, we could see a few hiding in the covered wagon, another behind a barrel in front of the saloon and two more at a table in *The Cantina*, hiding in plain sight, even miming eating with their silverware even though the placemat in front of them was empty. Beside them was the couple Nora had predicted would last 50 years and, for some reason, I knew she was right. Even though one could tell the relationship was new—the man's ears were red with rising blood pressure, the woman laughed at unfunny jokes—they were carbon copies of each other in different genders. That is not to say they looked alike, their ethnicities differed, but the affectation each carried while the other talked indicated a compatibility that cannot be quantified. Perhaps the presence of this attribute, or lack thereof, was the methodology for Nora's predictions. I considered asking her but spared myself. Eventually, Gabe's Flamethrowers filtered past as well as some Ocean Sidewinders, including Nora's nemesis.

"Another W for the Ocean Side*WIN*ders," Joe Kline said.

"Don't forget to prep your dad for my booty call tonight," Nora said.

Gabe intervened before tempers escalated, and I paid the bill and walked out with Nora, making sure to give Mr. Kline plenty of space. We walked toward the parking lot, past the Old Town bank and the church and the yellow lanterns of the saloon where a zebra-painted donkey ate alfalfa, arriving in the parking lot. Nora got in the truck and Gabe turned to me.

"Listen, I know you didn't come out here to donate to a library. If you wanna meet up and talk about whatever really brought you out tonight, I'd be happy to do that."

Nora honked and Gabe took the hint and handed me a business card then got in the truck. He turned the engine on and backed out of the parking lot.

⧗

The following week, I visited the maquiladora. Curators awaited my training at stations along the newly created eleventh row. Paco had ordered in the plyboard cubicles the previous week and had hired his nephew to put them together. One of the Recruiters, meanwhile, had managed getting another 10 wheelchairs from two different local hospitals, saving us a few hundred dollars. The trainees crowded around one cubicle as I talked them through the basics, like what to do with a request relating to torture, then showed them how to search efficiently, emphasizing the importance of trusting one's instinct and warning against dwelling too long on a single memory. I told them never to keep a Creative under for more than 60 minutes, pointing to the digital timer that turned on when the computer booted up. I repeated this instruction three times.

"Why?" someone asked.

"After 60 minutes, we lose the capacity to curate RAM and there are consequences if we surpass 60 minutes. Therefore, make sure to end at 55 minutes just to be safe."

Headquarters had given me this explanation and I'd found it sufficient at the time. I had done so many trainings by that point I forgot that this rule feels arbitrary when you first encounter it; forgotten the curiosity about what happened at minute 61; forgotten there was a time when ending the session at 55 minutes wasn't muscle memory.

Paco handed me a cup of coffee from the machine he'd installed in the corner of the warehouse. The coffee was always too strong and left a layer of silt at the bottom of the paper cups we drank from. I tried diluting it with creamer one time, but Paco looked appalled, taking it as a personal affront for some reason, so from then on, I drank it black and didn't complain.

A new Curator asked if there was a shortcut for finding sexual RAM given the volume of requests. I plugged in a hard drive of assorted memories we used for training purposes that were divided into five categories: Love, Travel, Pain, Violence, Spectacle—each Curator coding RAM as one of these categories based on the primary emotion and/or content. I clicked the Home button on the keyboard then opened the *Travel* folder and filled the screen with the most recent RAM—a couple with a two-year-old walking on the beach—then demonstrated how to use context clues.

"The child looks to be about two-years-old, correct? Press Control-F and type in a date two years and nine months before the time stamp on this RAM to approximate the time the Creative was engaged in intercourse. Given that it led to conception, the Creative will likely have some recollection."

The mechanics of Curation could be learned in a day, but the refinement of the process continued in perpetuum, even for me. I was embarrassed during each training because it was evident that our procedures were composed to solve a momentary problem at one point yet had calcified with repetition and became Standard Operating Procedure. Control-F-ing was one example. Compounding this problem was that the software had not developed as quickly as Headquarters had anticipated, so Curators were still using outdated methods like tapping arrow keys. I knew there was a plan for upgrading it, but I don't know what came of that.

Another Curator asked what to do if they did not come upon the RAM the client sought, even after a thorough search. I opened the Help Form and instructed them to describe the RAM needed and select SUBMIT, which sent a notification to other Curators who were instructed to keep watch for the elusive memory among their respective Creatives in addition to the requests from their own clients.

"In special cases, you can send these directly to me by pressing 'Send to Admin' in the lower righthand corner of the Help Form. Special cases include memories of funerals in Tijuana – something we will go into more depth in our next training," I said.

"Why?" one Curator, the type of person who sat in the front row of class, asked.

"Headquarters mandates it."

"But why?"

"I do not have supplemental information at this time."

This was a primary weapon in my non-response arsenal and yielded 90% effectiveness, including this occasion. I remember my inquisitiveness about this strange aberration was strong for the first two weeks as a Curator then dissipated into normality afterward, feeling entirely logical now.

"Any further questions?"

"If you transfer a memory—" one trainee said before I cut her off.

"From now on get in the habit of calling it Random Access Memory please or the abbreviated RAM."

The asker looked to the trainees for some form of affirmation, but none was given. She was plump and friendly like a human Christmas ornament. She continued her question.

"If you transfer ... RAM of ... sex, um, will the recipient feel love with it?"

"Please clarify."

Her cheeks reddened as she thought how to rephrase her question.

"Do memories come with emotions?

I explained how the memories would be encoded by the client's own brain as his, assimilating into the memory bank through transference. This was the simplest distillation of the process. Then I used my token example—a scandal involving a journalist who interviewed families displaced by a Category 5 hurricane in Cambodia then reported about "her" experience surviving the hurricane when it was revealed to be the experience of her Cambodian interviewees. She lived there but was in a different part of the country at the time the hurricane hit. Neuroscientists absolved her because of the same phenomenon that makes Memory Curation viable—our actual memories, and those we identify with but don't physically experience, meld over time. In short, I told the trainees, when a person's memory is embedded in me, "he" becomes "I" – what happened to him becomes what happened to me.

I concluded the training and they looked to one another in confusion. Paco always waited a half-hour after trainings before dismissing them so they could corroborate their understanding of the process with each other. I checked my watch and saw it was time to meet Gabe for the batting practice we had arranged after our meeting the previous week. I ordered a car that picked me up and took me through the express lane at the port of entry, avoiding the queue that had piled up. A headache settled into the back of my neck as the car passed through the mechanical arm that rose when my passport and facial profile were scanned. The car merged onto the 5-North where it coasted several miles then again onto the 8-East which branched toward Mission Valley – the geographical center of the region and known as the San Diego equivalent of flyover country. The car pulled into a parking lot in front of a small amusement park under a pink and purple sky. I knew that gaining Gabe's trust was the gateway to gaining Nora's, which is why I was outside a near-insolvent theme park at seven p.m. on a Wednesday. Gabe got out of his park ranger truck when I arrived and proceeded with his door-handle routine before hoisting his bat over his shoulder and walking toward me. Near the front entrance was a large batting cage where you could pay to hit in your own partitioned box and have pitching machines hurl baseballs toward you. A giant net hung over a dozen machines, keeping the balls from hitting the climbing gym it neighbored. The light of the *Bat Shack* with the token dispenser was still on, a chubby attendant perched behind the counter scrolling on his phone.

"Workin' hard or hardly workin'?" Gabe said when we reached him. His nametag said PHIL and his drooping eyes conveyed the same passive acquiescence I felt as he handed Gabe the keys and let himself out. Gabe took a bucket of dimpled softballs and led me to the middle of the batting cage, explaining how they did not have any machines for slow-pitch, while he eased into one of his middle-aged man stretches.

Gabe unraveled an extension cord and connected it with a halogen light he found in the shack, ferrying it out to the middle partition so he could see the pitches coming, then put on his batting gloves meticulously, left hand, then right, fidgeting with the Velcro straps before settling them along his wrists and touching each corner of the box with the tip of his bat.

I was not sure if I was supposed to underhand or baseball throw so I did a little of both—shot-putting it to the plate. He smiled, shook his head, and told me not to be ashamed to throw underhand. I lobbed several that fell short of the plate then, after ten or fifteen like this, tossed hittable pitches, one of which shot over my head, making me fall on the bucket and spill its contents over the uneven concrete. Gabe made no reaction as I collected the softballs back into the bucket. Eventually, he began hitting them to the corners of the batting cage, grunting as he did.

"So how do you know my sister?" he said, swinging and connecting, sending another just past my head.

"I just met her."

"How'd you meet her?"

"I was googling libraries in Tijuana and hers came up. I was motivated to donate from my strong belief in reviving the community from the grassroots by supporting the arts."

He knelt and adjusted the height of his socks to make sure they were the same length on his shins then picked up his bat and nodded and I threw the next one which he sent speeding past my head.

"Doesn't pass the sniff test."

I nodded, pretending to know what that meant, as he

exchanged his bat for a water bottle and drank until it was half-empty. I needed to modulate my approach, the standard corporate-speak proving ineffective for this audience. Perhaps a more personal angle? More self-effacing?

"Nora never brings people to my games."

I did not respond, deciding to throw the last ball instead, which he sent into the darkness. He grabbed an extra bucket and walked off to the right and began collecting the balls and I did the same in the opposite direction.

"We're close ya know, Nora and me," he said across the cage. Every couple seconds were punctuated with the sound of a hard rubber softball dropping into the bucket. He poured his half in with mine, then walked up the incline to the box and picked up his bat and we resumed our roles for another round. Then another. And another. By the end of it, I could manage getting most of the pitches knee-high around the plate. He grew quieter with each passing round. We collected the last round and deposited them in the shed which he locked up while I walked to the parking lot overhung with streetlamps like concerned parents. A light breeze blew dirt across the asphalt.

"This isn't about a library," Gabe said, beside me now.

I responded by nodding slightly, a tactic I reserved for occasions when the conversationalist had a hunch they wanted to indulge. I provided space for the hunch then improvised from there, using the hunch as a cue for my response. In this instance, I decided whatever theory he postulated, I would confirm because that would create a more collaborative narrative which we could maneuver together.

"You want to date my sister."

Despite my resolution to confirm any theory, I hesitated, then realized my hesitation was beneficial given it substantiated the untrue, but useful narrative of an insecure suitor approaching a protective older brother to ask permission to date his attractive younger sister.

"That's correct."

If I were to pretend to pursue Nora in order to connect with Gabe, this would provide opportunities for regular meetings, dating advice, and, potentially, the exchange of useful intimate information.

"Have you eaten?" he said, watching a spotlight search the sky near the arena off the freeway exit.

"I have not."

Responding that you have not eaten was always the correct answer. No one appreciates being made to eat alone or to feel like he or she is forcing the other to eat just for accompaniment; plus, food provided a point of connection that always helped restart conversation if it had flattened.

We got in the car and he pushed the ignition, switched to driverless, and said *Wendy's*. We arrived at the drive-thru ten minutes, two freeways, and three stoplights later and ordered chicken sandwiches/fries/burgers/milkshakes, then parked in the nearest spot after receiving the food. Gabe ate fries five-at-a-time with no ketchup because the packets were too hard for him to open. In between mouthfuls, Gabe started opening up.

"I don't usually eat like this."

He looked to me, unconvinced that I was convinced, which was correct.

"Honestly, I don't. Usually it's something much healthier, like sushi, do you like sushi?" he said, his lisp inflecting the s's.

"I do."

"You'd like this then—there are these restaurants in Japan where all of the tables are in a circle and they have this conveyer belt running past every table with all sorts of sushi. And when the sushi that you want comes along, you just take it off the conveyer belt. Wild, huh?"

"That sounds efficient."

Gabe poured hand sanitizer on his fingers before opening the wrapper of his chicken sandwich, offering me some which I obliged.

"And there's this other restaurant built right next to a trash compactor—ya know, like the one in Star Wars. There's a big window where you can see the trash being compacted as you eat. Crazy huh?"

I realized this was the perfect opportunity, given Japan's reputation with technological innovation and how the West marvels at it—Gabe's comments being Exhibit A and B. Should Nora show interest in donating RAM, Gabe having a vague awareness of the technology would not hurt.

"Have you heard of Japanese firms conducting Memory Curation?" I said.

"What?"

"It is a new technology that allows for the collection and deposit of memories from one person to another person."

"Memories? Actual memories? Personal, human memories?"

"That is my understanding."

"How's that even work?"

"They created software."

This remained an uncontestable point with anyone whose mind went entirely blank when they heard the word *software* and I correctly predicted Gabe was among them. He paused, his half-eaten sandwich between his hands.

"Why would anyone want another person's memories?" Gabe asked.

I asked the same question to my brother 10 years ago, when he was working on the very first version of this software. We were on the phone, talking about Formula 1, and I asked him about his senior project, the reason he'd missed the last Thanksgiving and Christmas. He explained the concept and how it worked and I asked the same question.

"Why would I want someone else's memories?"

"After the transfer from them to you, their memories become your own. You can't tell the difference."

"Still—why would I want that?"

There was a long, drawn-out groan. Jordan detested elaboration. He viewed conversations as mutual monologues occurring on separate planes—ships passing in the night. Therefore, he seldom elaborated on anything, ever. But this time he did, to humor me, I guess.

"Last year in my marketing class we were given a prompt at the start of the semester: Make a product that all Americans would want. That was it. That's where this idea began."

"I don't understand."

"What do all Americans want, Sol?"

"I don't know."

"Everything. We want everything. Why live one life when you could live a thousand?"

His words echoed in my mind as I turned to Gabe, the several seconds of reliving this conversation with Jordan in my mind doubling as cover for careful consideration of his question before responding with a shrug. Gabe ate the rest of his sandwich and folded the wrapper into neat quarters.

"Ready to go?"

I concluded that Gabe probably did not consider the technology real in the same way we do not consider natural disasters in faraway countries real. I stuffed my unfinished dinner into the paper bag, but Gabe stopped me before I could find the nearest trashcan. Behind the center console were three containers labeled: *Compost, Plastic, Paper*—each big enough to fit a shoe. He scraped the beef that was stuck to the wrapper and nubs of fries into the first, put the wrappers in the second, and the receipt and brown bag into the third, closing each with a snap.

He turned the car on and chose the self-driving mode. We rolled out of the parking lot, his lifted truck towering over the other cars, my eyes following the steering wheel as it rotated. Whenever I closed my eyes in a car at night, my first thought is of a small child in a giant cardboard box and a father shaking it in different directions pretending it was a spaceship navigating asteroids. I couldn't tell if this was my memory or someone else's.

"How would you be a positive influence on my sister?" Gabe said.

I had forgotten that taking this approach would mean answering questions a protective brother would undoubtedly ask, with every answer being met with scrutiny. My silence operated as contemplative thought. Finally, he turned toward me expecting a response.

"She would be less alone."

This was the only answer I could come up with at the time. He did not brush it off, so I must have touched upon something. Perhaps he thought a new relationship might do her good, even if it was one that did not last very long. The truck coasted off the freeway and stopped at a stoplight in the left-turn lane. One block up, a freight train passed so slow it could be outrun and Gabe turned on the stereo and played a song with an operatic singer accompanied by a resonant guitar and a lilting accordion—each instrument one-half of a loving relationship come to an end. It was a famous Mexican ballad that was passed down from prior generations, according to Gabe, a song that was played often in the orphanage he grew up in. The song lasted until the last carriage of the train passed and the long arm of the railroad crossing rose. The truck took the hills with ease as we climbed toward my apartment, glimpsing Balboa for an instant.

"I appreciate you asking if you can take my sister out, it's, well, it's the right thing to do," he said, shaking my hand.

"Of course," I said and got out. He U-turned and I watched until he disappeared around the bend, then sat on the curb with that strange song echoing in my mind for an untold amount of time.

CHAPTER 5

Balboa Park attracted its usual mix of tourists expecting something more and locals content with what was. The regulars took their respective stations: the didgeridoo player with his straw hat, the refugee parents who sent their third-grader to plead for cash, the Atheist tent and the Pentecostal tent, each with loud banners and no visitors. White flies caught sunlight and drifted above the grass. Mr. Bray sat on the bench under a jacaranda tree across from the fountain. I sat beside him and watched him smooth wrinkles out of his khakis. A Quinceañera photoshoot unfolded before us—boys in man-sized suits formed a confused semi-circle around the girl as the photographer gave instructions and made adjustments.

"You don't have the information I need."

Mr. Bray's cheeks had acne scars that looked like crumpled rags. His statements were leading, as if he all he wanted was to hear the tone, rather than the content, of my responses.

"No."

"Tell me why that is."

"Building trust is the first step."

"It's taking you longer this time for some reason."

The slap of a skateboard reverberated throughout the plaza. The skater cursed and wiped the hair out of his eyes, tucking it under a black beanie while his friend filmed, kneeling down to capture the trick from a different angle. Mr. Bray winced at the sound of each attempt. He called them over, but they ignored him at first. He reached into his pocket and pulled out to two $100 bills and told them that he would invest in their skating careers if they pissed off somewhere else. They walked over, trying to be nonchalant, and took the money. They exchanged hi-fives as they walked away comparing their legal tender. Mr. Bray slipped his feet out of his shoes. His toenails were yellow and cracked, his heel pink like raw meat.

"This business of ours is a curious one, isn't it?"

"I suppose so."

Replies like this, I found, had a high degree of success because they reflect the comment back to the speaker, making him feel listened to while providing space to carry on his thought, like the artful non-answers from a White House Press Secretary.

"We pay such a premium for memories when they only capture a tiny proportion of lived experience. They are ephemeral. Echoes. Life becomes like paying to see a concert but only hearing every fifth song from behind a fence. And yet we do it because what other option do we have? Once our memories go, well then, you may as well go with them. But why is that the case? Why hang our humanity on such a thin string?"

He turned to me for a response, but I did not have one.

"Tell me—what percentage of the details, feelings, smells, sights, sounds, do you think you retain as memories?"

"It is impossible to calculate."

"Guess then."

"Two percent."

"And that two percent—what is it composed of?"

"Points of heightened clarity."

"Jesus, you are a piece of work. I've never heard anyone talk like you," he said, rubbing the heel of the foot he'd hoisted over his other leg. "You mean highs and lows, right? Have many highs do you have then?"

"Not a large amount."

"Mostly lows then."

"I suppose."

"So most of the life you've retained is composed of suffering. And we're conditioned to think that our memories are valuable because they are all we have and that those memories, even the ones of suffering, somehow build the person that we are—isn't that correct?"

"Yes."

I found that giving too many neutral answers (maybe, perhaps, I suppose) produce the impression of ineffectuality, so I interspersed a healthy amount of binary yes and no answers to propel the dialogue forward, which worked marginally well.

"So, if I were a particularly memorable person, I would be giving you more of your life—even if those memories were negative—isn't that the case?"

"Yes."

"According to this inquiry, then, the suboptimal life is not one of transgression, malevolence or even sadism—because these behaviors will cause pain for others to convert to memories that will enable personal growth and fuel meaning in life. Rather, the most suboptimal is the inert life—entirely complacent, forgettable, living wallpaper. Isn't that true? Because the complacent man never impacts the life of the other—negatively or positively—therefore never endows the other with memory. Whereas those who inflict pain on others give them something to remember, to learn from, to explore the depths of self, correct?"

He smiled, the Venus flytrap opening once more.

An old couple in matching sun hats sat on the adjacent bench. They discussed funerals as chunks of bread dropped from their fingers onto the granite stones for the birds that waddled over. Jerry's was best, they agreed, but Georgia's was a close second.

They made predictions about Fred's upcoming one.

"Was he cremated?" the man asked.

"It's a graveside ceremony," she said.

"So they're going to bury the jar?" the man said, tearing a piece from the loaf and passing it to her. Mr. Bray turned toward them.

"What would you say if I offered you each a hundred dollars to feed pigeons somewhere else?"

"What would you say if I told you this is *public* pro-per-ty," the woman said.

"I realize that. So I'm offering you a business proposition to create a little more privacy for myself and my associate here. What do you say?"

"And just *where* are we supposed to go?" the woman said, her grip tightening on the bread.

"Anywhere I can't hear you."

He removed another $200 from his billfold. The couple approached, unsure if the offer was real. The husband watched his wife's face convulse with an operatic internal struggle, before shaking her head and pulling him away toward the Botanic Garden.

"Nudge me when she comes back."

A few minutes later, I saw her marching toward us in her floral blouse and I nudged Mr. Bray who smiled as she snatched the cash without a word. Mr. Bray plucked a strand of grass under the bench and twisted it in his fingertips. Working with this demographic for a few years taught me when I could leave and when I could not. He was there, waiting for something, and I was meant to wait beside him. So we waited.

"Do you believe in God?" he said.

"I don't know, Mr. Bray."

He nodded and mumbled something I could not discern.

"I don't. But I believe in the Catholic Church. They verify

miracles, you see. It's well-documented. An institution that verifies the supernatural. Now *that* is something to believe in."

He paused ceremonially for me to respond with something that would allow him to continue his monologue, which I obliged.

"How so?"

"There were two men—born five hundred years apart—Juan Diego and Juan José Barragán Silva. Juan Diego was a peasant, married, devoted to family, revered the Virgin and so on and so forth. While caring for his uncle and performing his religious duties on the outskirts of what has become Mexico City, he encountered an apparition of the Virgin (of course) at dawn one day in late December. She told him to build a chapel in her honor. She returned to heal his uncle from the brink of death, heal an Indian of an arrow wound and so on and so forth. None of that particularly interests me. What interests me is Juan José Barragán Silva five hundred years later."

Food trucks parked along the promenade to our right, the smell of BBQ and falafel wafting toward us. Tourists descended on the plaza. Mr. Bray spread his arms along the top of the bench, his hand now just behind my neck.

"Juan José Barragán Silva was your typical twenty-year-old cokehead who attempted suicide by diving from a balcony thirty feet off the ground. Unfortunately for him, two things were not in his favor: one, he chose a balcony near the place of Juan Diego's encounter with the Virgin and, two, his mother was a prayerful woman who interceded on his behalf to that same saint, Juan Diego, to save her son from his own stupidity which caused the damage to his head, spine, and neck. And, apparently, the prayer worked! The church's bureaucrats gathered accounts from eyewitnesses, medical records, testimonies and sent them to the Congregation for the Causes of Saints in Rome. You see, they had an actual procedure for this! They passed it along to 'theological consultants' who examined the fall, the faith of the mother, the recovery and *eleven years* after the event the miracle was in fact acknowledged by the Pope as a miracle." Mr. Bray leaned back on the bench and formed a web with his hands that he put his head into. "Now, darling, what is the moral of that story?"

"Use a more effective means of suicide."

Mr. Bray laughed, then burrowed his thumb into the tissue beneath my shoulder blade.

"The *other* moral of the story is that even if God Almighty comes down from Heaven to perform a miracle, it is only real if we verify it."

All I wanted was to go home but I knew decorum dictated I entertain the client until he dismissed me. A couple feet from our bench, a toddler looked in awe at the purple flowers of the blooming jacarandas that covered the city in the spring. She picked the fallen flowers off the ground, but these had wilted and browned and lost their appeal while the ones that captivated her remained out-of-reach.

"It's been three months, what do you have to show for it?" said Mr. Bray, sitting forward in his seat, his khakied knee touching mine. His eyes had a faint yellow tinge I had not noticed before—the pupil smaller than a sighted person's.

"I am making progress."

"Make more. I'm running out of time."

This was my only mistake of the conversation, for it was Mr. Bray who determined whether or not there was progress being made. I usually never said the first response that came to mind; I preferred the third response, or, ideally, the fourth. After that many revisions, the response was tempered, fine-tuned.

"You have feelings for her?"

"No."

He placed two fingers on the pulse of my neck and waited a

few moments before relaxing his hand back on my shoulder.

"There does seem to be something different with this one, doesn't there?"

"I don't know what you mean."

"Of course you don't. You're a follower, Sol. You followed your brother into this profession and now that he's gone, you're lost."

"You knew him?"

He unfolded his walking stick that looked like a candy cane, rolling the end of it along the ground like a blade over a sharpening stone.

"Tell me what I asked you to do so I can confirm we understand each other."

I described the task to him as he described it to me the first time I met him.

"To facilitate the Curation of currently unspecified memories from Nora Rincón to you."

"That's correct. And every month that goes by and this doesn't happen, the consequences increase in severity. Understand?"

"It would help me conduct my work if I knew the type of memory you are looking for, Mr. Bray."

Whenever I made eye contact with him I had to remind myself he could not see me, his dim blue eyes at odds with his potent voice.

"She has memories of a place I need to go and a man I need to meet. An old, crippled Mexican man."

"Is it possible for me to ask her for the coordinates of the place and the name of the man you are seeking, Mr. Bray?"

"No." He got up from his seat and straightened his legs. "Don't waste any more of my time. There will be consequences if you do."

He began walking toward the bell tower, his right leg dragging behind his left, sunlight filtering through the leaves of the jacaranda canopy above him. He walked between the line of food trucks, tourists parting for him as he did, course-correcting with his cane around the planters and the tables of the main square and down the hallway past the didgeridoo player, the bell tower, eventually reaching the sidewalk of the bridge toward the dog park and his apartment beyond. I sat on the stairs in front of the fountain and anticipated every eventuality so that none of it would be unanticipated therefore rendering Mr. Bray's threat harmless. Then I thought about the cowboy with the gasmask I had seen the last time I was in this park and my fear returned, because sometimes unpredictable events just happen.

I considered how to gain Nora's trust, she being the most difficult person to anticipate in recent memory. But Gabe was much less so. I could read him. Perhaps his religious faith also meant faith in people, i.e. me. My last session with Gabe revealed that he thought I was seeking his permission to date Nora even though I did not display feelings for her. Running with this narrative, however, allowed me a shortcut to friendship with Gabe who saw himself as simultaneously protecting his sister and vetting me—both highly appealing to his temperament.

To better appropriate this persona, I created online dating profiles on various platforms, fabricating parts of my personality for each profile in accordance with the normative practice per platform. In one, I emphasized being a career-driven professional who is curious about people. In another, I emphasized love of travel and dogs—including photos of other people's travel and dogs. In the final profile I accentuated my taste in wine and food, accompanying these with photos meant to evoke an air of mystery. Once these profiles were made, I texted Gabe, explaining how I was "at a loss" in my approach to dating and how to connect with Nora, using these profiles as evidence for my claim. He responded with a simple "I hear ya man!" and some friendly emojis designed to put me at ease, which, oddly, worked. I saw the meditative dots that indicated he was typing but no message came. This happened a few times. Then, finally, he told me to come down to the estuary for a ride-along and he'd coach me through it. Everyone likes to think themselves a matchmaker. I wondered if this invitation arose from the inclination to give quiet, severely introverted individuals the benefit of the doubt. Perhaps he saw me as a blank slate on which he projected a wholesomeness that had more to do with him than me.

By the time Mr. Bray left, it was late afternoon and my monthly maquiladora visit awaited. I called a car and took it south toward the border. I felt like a storm chaser as the freeway led me directly toward the dense clouds huddled above the hills much of Tijuana was built on. When I arrived at the maquiladora, it began to rain.

Paco met me outside and we watched the bulldozers and cranes at the construction site below press on through the intermittent rain, hoping it would cease. Inside, we did the rounds, checking-in with the team leads on each row as they traded insults about the leaderboard—the prize on offer from Headquarters being day-passes to a nearby waterpark. I started an advanced training with new Curators, the last session they had to complete prior to being certified for Curation. This session covered anomalies, special circumstances, and general Q&A. It ended with me supervising their first Curation. Each time I facilitated a training, I code-switched to what could be called a peppier, more outspoken iteration of myself, one I was able to access less and less as each month passed for some reason I could not place.

"Can anyone tell me a primary example of RAM—remember that's Random Access Memories—that would fall under Special Circumstances?" I said, looking at the ten new Curators. Several muted seconds passed until one of them, a young man fifty pounds overweight, half-raised his hand and I called on him.

"Something about funerals?" he said.

"Correct. Any RAM of a funeral or a cemetery visit of any kind gets placed in the folder titled *Special Circumstances* which is on every single computer."

"What happens with those?"

"Administration reviews them," I said, giving him the answer I was given.

During their first Curation, Curators will usually get a migraine or nausea or, in severe cases, vertigo, because they do not understand what they are looking at. Some of the debriefing reports from when the product was in beta indicated that Curators treated the job like any work, nothing more, which helped the process go smoothly. Paco funneled in Creatives to the row of new Curators I had just finished training. Creatives were generally happy before Curation because of the compensation they received, but Paco's new recruits looked exhausted, inert. He deciphered my confusion.

"Ilegales," he said.

This clarification prompted me to instruct Curators to open the second drawer of their desks and remove the form we used to process this category of Creative. Due to the arrangement the company made with the relevant authorities, we were permitted to curate all RAM these Creatives gathered during their unauthorized time in the U.S. (including American territories). Each Curator read the form's instructions to the Creative while affixing a yellow wristband which informed us who would bypass Pay Distribution. The Creatives signed and the process proceeded normally from there.

We took a break and Paco and I had our customary Modelo outside, the rain abating for its duration. The construction workers below us churned the soil, digging a trench with a backhoe. Neither of us said very much as we rolled our bottles down the hillside and ventured through the roll-up door once again. In the row nearest us, I saw an American in a metallic blue suit with a platinum tie at the end of the row. He sat in the wheelchair beside the paunchy Curator. I watched the teenager bite his bottom lip as he began arranging the gel pads on the gentleman's head. The kid pulled up the man's file on his computer, then looked to me, caught with an anomalous case when he was only learning the job like a new waiter serving the restaurant owner.

"Good to see you, Mr. Grass."

"Sol," he said with a nod.

Sweat beaded the teenager's forehead as I modulated how to approach the problem of explaining the situation to him and communicating the instructions clearly without divulging any unnecessary information. Mr. Grass closed his eyes. I watched the Curators untangle the knotted wires of the gel pads while their Creatives sat in the wheelchairs beside them. After another minute or so, most of them had managed to get the pads affixed in the correct places, all except the young Curator with Mr. Grass, which provided an instructional moment.

"The gel pads are affixed in the wrong areas," I said, pointing to Mr. Grass's neck and forehead, where the Curator had placed the pads. The others looked over from their cubicles, their Creatives already under, RAM slowly populating each of their screens in squares like document icons. The teenager turned red as Mr. Grass showed his annoyance.

I unstuck each of the five gel pads and reattached them to the correct areas of the head that covered the parts of the brain where memories are stored—amygdala (direct middle on each side of the head), hippocampus (directly beneath and slightly behind the amygdala), and the neocortex (midway between the top of the head and the neck)—all while Mr. Grass chastised me about mussing his hair. Finally, he went under. RAM populated the screen and cohered into a timeline of his life that our software composed based on age estimates of the memories.

"What is he here for?" the Curator asked.

I thought about the real answer to this question while composing a vaguely evasive one to say. The real answer was that Mr. Grass acquires memories of new software ideas he then pitches to venture capitalists in Silicon Valley. He doesn't understand them well enough to pitch if we don't embed the memory of the concept itself. He has a rotation of ten-to-fifteen developers in Tijuana he sources ideas from—most of whom are still in college and think of these ideas in-between sessions of getting high and playing Minecraft. After the college students come in and we curate, we keep the memories in one place, in anticipation of Mr. Grass's next visit. The software concepts that Mr. Grass fails to find VC funding for, he then sells back to us, which we in turn sell to different entrepreneurs in Tijuana. A handful of successful start-ups were founded this way.

"He's here for business," I ended up saying, calling an experienced Curator from two rows over to replace the teenager once the instructional moment was over.

The new Curators started filtering through the memories, hovering over the squares that contained an individual memory which showed them a small segment, like a preview. I watched him open one—a memory of a woman smiling, raising her chin, all of which lasted only a few seconds.

"Why's it just end? Shouldn't there be more?" the paunchy Curator asked, hovering over us.

"Memories are not videos. They are more like gifs, like impressions, little vignettes of a moment. You might find the entirety of a memory as just one of these moments, just one vignette, or a succession of these moments. Think about your own memories, do they work different than what you see on the screen before you?"

The group nodded in unison and resumed. Paco set out little bottles of shampoo we supplied each Creative to wash out the residual stickiness of the gel pads. After he placed the last bottle on the desk at the end of the row, Paco told me to follow him, a smile breaking across his lips. He brought me to the Lost & Found locker in the corner that contained items we'd accrued over the last couple years—tube socks, a toy badge, a yellowed retainer, headphones with the foam torn out, a leather watch that still worked, various sunglasses, and lots of shoes: Converse, flip flops, boots, Skechers, platform shoes, slip-ons, loafers, running shoes. Paco rummaged through until he found a selfie stick and attached his phone and started taking photos of everything he could find in the maquiladora except himself, apparently not understanding the concept of the device.

"Wait-wait-wait," he said. "Close your eyes."

I heard the magazine from his assault rifle unhinge and the snap of the chamber, then the sound of duct tape peeling.

"Keep 'em shut, boss."

I heard something unravel from a spool. After another minute, he finally let me open my eyes. He had run a line of string from the trigger of the duct-taped selfie stick to that of the unloaded rifle. He pointed the gun barrel at me, the phone affixed to the edge, and pulled the trigger, taking a photo of my blank expression. He howled with laughter then pointed at the diesel canisters next to the generators—*click*. The routers perched on the cart beside them—*click*. The ATM that disbursed the payments—*click*. The Curator next to him who dismissed him with a flick of the hand—*click*. Each Creative in the row nearest us—*click, click, click, click, click, click, click, click, click, click.*

I spotted Uno—the old woman with strap-on shoes seated one row away from us. We had a long history together. She always haggled over payment but remained our most loyal Creative, she being the very first, which led to my brother giving her that nickname. Jordan valued her for some reason he never specified, because he had assigned me to personally curate dozens of her memories, so I've seen every lover she has ever had. Her different-colored eyes emblazoned themselves on our memories and I noticed most of the Curators knew her even if they didn't curate her. She was under, the Curator seated beside her, one I didn't recognize. The small clock atop the computer was blank, which was unusual, so I walked over and noticed the screen was blank as well. No blue lights glowed on the pads adhered to Uno's wrinkled skin.

"What's wrong?" I asked.

The Curator looked at me and nodded, then restarted his computer.

"No, what is wrong with her? Why is the Curation not happening?"

He gave a thumbs up and smiled. I called to Paco.

"What's up, boss?" he said, the levity from his prank still audible in his voice.

"Ask him why the Curation is not happening."

Paco asked him in Spanish and he gave the same thumbs up and nod he gave me.

"He's deaf," the Curator next to him said without looking up from her screen.

"How long has the Creative been unconscious?"

She shrugged.

"You think she's been under too long?" Paco said.

"I don't know. All I know is that when I turn the clock back on, it can't be stopped at zero. It should've stopped at five minutes."

I hesitated, looking at the black button on the side of the clock that would restore the timer. I rubbed the sweat off my hands and put my finger on the button, then pressed it…

00:00.00

Paco put his fingers in front of her nose then checked her pulse—nothing.

"I'll take care of it boss," he said, patting my shoulder.

He grabbed the Curator out of his seat and dragged him up the stairs and out the front. I sat in a chair beside her, staring at the painted eyebrows of the woman. Paco walked back down 15 minutes later and rolled her to the back entrance, humming as he waited for the door to roll up. I walked up the stairs and out the front entrance, past the lobby, and onto the cul-de-sac. The deaf Curator was nowhere to be seen. A black pick-up truck was parked there, gate open, one wheel on the curb.

Paco came around from the back, the dead woman still in the wheelchair that he rolled to the truck. He motioned me over. Uno's body slumped across the truck's gate as Paco handed me a massive burlap bag and told me to hold it open and I did. He shoved Uno in head-first in one swift motion, zipped the bag up, covered it with a tarp, and drove east as the night descended with the color of a bruise.

CHAPTER 6

I started calling Nora on the phone. Our conversations always began with her mentioning some new life change, like shaking hands with her left instead of her right just to observe how it made others feel. I learned that if I simply misstated a fact about whatever current obsession she had—which at the time was bowling—she would correct me with a 20-minute elaboration. She started calling me as well, her tone always sounding as if she had tried everybody else in her phone and I was a last resort. She knew I was not a normal person which gave her the space to talk about things not-normal people talk about, like why there are not more black swimmers or what it would feel like to breastfeed puppies.

I found that I was able to sleep a full four hours after these conversations which made me call her more and more, not because I was attracted to Nora but because I was guaranteed sleep afterward. These warm nights were ushered in by a sky whose colors were soft and blue—nights where darkness was comforting, like a polite guest whose arrival I expected. Conversations with Nora began to erode my metric for determining how much time to devote to a conversation. Usually, it looked something like the following:

$$\frac{\text{Valuable info they have (ten scale)}}{\text{Time required (in hours) to divulge info}} - \text{Personality drawbacks} = \text{Time devoted}$$

The average conversation would score something like this:

$$\frac{\text{Valuable info they have: 4.5}}{\text{Time required (in hours): .3}} - \begin{matrix}\text{Personality}\\ \text{Drawbacks: 2}\end{matrix} = \text{13 min.}$$

Nora confounded this metric by mixing the valuable information she had with the superfluous, making it difficult to parse between them. Her personality drawbacks were countless and immeasurable, thereby creating a new paradigm that nullified my equation. Curiosity about this unique method of dismantling my conversational S.O.P. compounded with Mr. Bray's task made meeting Nora in-person a priority, which led to visiting a café in Zona Centro, the kind of place that asks if you want whole or oat or almond milk in your coffee. The pretext I invented for the meeting related to an itemization of the places my contribution to the library would be allocated.

"Thank you for meeting with me today. I'm looking forward to discussing the specifics of how my financial contribution will uplift and empower the next generation."

She sipped a cappuccino, eyebrows sine waving. Tall women climbed the stairs behind her, leading to somewhere above us that required high heels; they greeted a man who wore an expensive watch and led them inside.

"You don't understand anything about working with people, do you?"

"I've had quality outcomes with clients in the past."

"How come you never answer questions with more than, like, one sentence?"

"One-sentence responses are usually sufficient."

"According to whom?"

"Shall we discuss the itemization of renovations for the library?"

I sensed that Nora was uncomfortable with corporatized language, so I increased its use in my vernacular in order to create an opportunity for cultural exchange i.e., her offering to help me with a perceived deficiency so that she did not feel the sole beneficiary in our partnership, an opportunity she capitalized on quicker than I anticipated.

"When's the last time you talked with a woman your age?" she said, arms crossed.

"Today."

"No, no, no—I don't count."

"I'm unsure."

"Don't worry, dude—I'll teach you how to connect with a fellow human being." She clasped her hands together and leaned forward, as if presenting a new concept to a boardroom. "Step one—ask me a question."

"What kind of music do you listen to?"

This question generally proved effective because everyone (except me) listens to music, which provides an easy talking point.

"Wu Tang. Step two—ask a follow-up question."

"I'm sorry?"

"Like ask *another* question."

"No—the musician you mentioned, I'm not familiar."

"Wu Tang. Wu. Tang. Clan. You've never heard of Wu Tang?" she said, making a W sign with her two hands, thumbs touching.

"No."

"RZA? GZA?"

I shook my head.

"Method Man?"

"No."

"Raekwon? Ghostface Killah? Inspectah Deck?"

I shrugged.

"U-God? Masta Killa? Cappadonna?"

"I do not know any of these people."

"Ol' Dirty Bastard a.k.a. ODB a.k.a. best member of Wu Tang?"

"No."

"What the fuck?" she crossed her arms. "Alright, whatever. Your homework is to look them up. They are pioneers of hip hop. *The* pioneers of hip hop."

"Okay."

"Step three—ask a specific question about a different topic."

"What do you do in your free time?" Another fail-safe question.

"Are you reading these from a survey?" Nora said. "Let me qualify that last step: ask me something specific *to me*—haven't you learned *anything* about me in the past few months?"

I considered this question for a few moments while I sipped my latte. Nora reminded me of someone I couldn't place and knew I never would.

"Why do you fundraise for a library?"

She slapped the table, spilling her cappuccino.

"Yes! Ok, so I've thought a lot about that myself and the conclusion I've come to has to do with the After School Children—A.S.C.'s ..." she said, motioning with her fingers like a director telling the cameraman to keep rolling.

"Step four—follow up your original question with an insightful response that lets the person know you're paying attention then make a connection to your own life or ask another specific question."

"What does library fundraising have to do with the children you mentioned?"

"Where else can A.S.C.'s go when class ends and there's no programming for them after school? Me and my crew provide a space that is safe, has A/C, Wifi, and marginally comfortable seating, not to mention all the books if they are so inclined. Same goes for the homeless—who I call A.S.C.'s all-grown-up—where can they go?"

"To your library?"

"That's right. To my motherfuckin' library. You know what makes it one-of-a-kind?"

"I do not."

"Donate another five grand and I'll tell you."

"I will think about that offer."

A man wearing a John Deere hat pulled to the curb and sat with his Chevy idling, keeping his eyes on the rearview mirror until a Mercedes pulled even. He passed something in a black garbage bag window-to-window and the Mercedes sped off. Nora's eyes narrowed as she took a sip from her cup.

"Don't think I haven't noticed how on all our phone calls, I'm the one doing the heavy lifting. Do people usually let you get away with not opening up?"

"Yes."

Extroverts tend to think the minds of quiet people are as silent as their mouths, but my experience is much the opposite.

"Let's try this—I'll tell you something about me and you have to tell me the corresponding thing about you. For instance, if I said what I ate for breakfast this morning you'd have to tell me what you ate for breakfast."

"I didn't eat breakfast."

"Of course you didn't. So we'll start with our jobs instead—I nanny for families in La Jolla and run a badass library. Your turn."

"I am a Curator."

"You've said that before but what does it mean?"

"I am the Curator for a memory brokering firm in the San Diego-Tijuana region."

This was a gamble but—after my previous conversation with Mr. Bray—one that proved necessary.

She tapped her fingers on her lips as if they were piano keys. A group sped past on dirt-bikes, popping wheelies and flipping off drivers, the sound making the coffee drinkers wince at the engines' torque.

"You are the weirdest person I know," she said. "Are you a virgin?"

"I don't understand the question."

"So, when two people—"

"I understand the literal question but not the import of it."

"My God, you make everything sound very technical. Is that how you talk dirty?" she started laughing and I did not respond, which I realized exacerbated the awkwardness of my initial response. She made a face that indicated that she would not proceed to her next talking point until the previous one was addressed. Given my hesitation, she provided a conversational stopgap in the form of a mindread.

"You're wondering if I'm a virgin right now, aren't you?"

"No." I was.

"Wow," she said shaking her head. "I can't *believe* you."

She crossed her arms and turned away in a way I can only think to describe with the antiquated phrase *in a huff*. Those at the neighboring table looked over, anticipating good gossip.

"I apologize."

"Just kidding, *dude*, why would I be a virgin?" she said. "Should we go bowling?"

I said yes—not knowing if she was serious but indulging her either way—and we left the café and took side-streets that ran between apartments where laundry hung on patio railings, the shirts changing from t-shirts to long-sleeves to nothing at all as we walked toward the destination. She took us down another street where vintage Volkswagens were parked near the back entrance of a bowling alley with a ceiling so low that I kept fighting the instinct to hunch. Nora told the attendant her shoe size then walked over to the wooden jukebox while I paid for our shoes and rounds. She danced to a pop song I didn't recognize and adrenaline shot through me not because of her movement but because I realized I had never bowled.

She picked a black ball, glittered to look like a galaxy, and I picked one that fit my fingers despite the crack near the thumbhole. We chose an empty lane, our names preloaded to the screen which indicated it was Nora's turn first. She rolled the ball down the lane and got a strike on her first roll. I approached the line and dropped the ball on the lane, watching it roll into the right-hand trench then walked back to my seat as Nora shouted *Walk of SHAME* over and over while the TV above the lane ridiculed me with a knock-off Homer Simpson gutterballing. On her second roll, she got a spare then moonwalked back to her seat.

She watched as I tossed a gutterball that was met with another shaming. Her next shot arched, kissing the edge of the gutter then bending toward the center while her hands became finger pistols that shot down the pins as the ball tumbled through them. She blew the imaginary smoke from the tips of her fingers, then watched my attempt. I tried bending my legs at the correct angle to make the ball transfer from hand to lane without thudding, but the result was a diagonal line toward the gutter.

"You look like a stroke victim when you bowl, do you realize that?"

"No."

"More like a stroke victim suffering an aneurism."

"Okay."

She turned and glided into her next roll then turned back as nine pins leveled which resulted in a celebratory little dance.

"Maybe your lack of coordination would qualify as a disability and they'd give us one of those ramps that provide the perfect angle for your ball."

She finished her spare and I tossed my bowling ball trying to walk back before she could shame me, but she pointed with a look of disbelief as my ball was still rolling so I turned back in time to see the ball just miss the last pin on the righthand side. Nora's laughter could be heard two lanes over. This cycle repeated a few more times before the game ended. We sat at the restaurant counter afterward, each with a greasy burger and a basket of fries between us and she talked in-between ketchup dips.

"So what is it you really do? How do you afford all this expensive shit?" she said, pointing to my cufflinks.

"It would just be easier to show you my work than explain it to you."

"Is it some sort of—what's it called—currency trading company?"

"It's similar."

"Are you a Navy SEAL and you can't tell me?" she said, her voice lowering.

"I am not."

"Dude, it was a *joke*. Look at you—you really think anyone would mistake you for a Navy SEAL? Maybe if they needed, like, a guy who specializes in *squeezing* between aisles and reaching top shelves."

She took a bite of the burger she held in both hands while I cut mine into quadrants and ate each piece with a fork.

"Maybe when you show me your work it's something I could take a crack at. How hard could whatever you do really be? I could do with some part-time work for some of that *sultry* broccoli."

Her attention shifted to the telenovela on the TV. Tank-topped men shot pool across from us, a stack of bills on the corner pocket. The smell of old coffee and stale cheese wafted from the kitchen as I chewed the spongy sesame seed bun. She crumpled up her wrapper on the plastic tray and said goodbye to the cook and we walked outside, the sky awash in three-toned blue.

"Ya know, Gabe'd be too shy to admit it, but his church could really use some of your disposable humanitarian income as well." She shrugged. "Just a thought."

She crossed the street, singing a ballad that sounded like one passed down, striding down a side-street until she disappeared from view. I imagined Nora as a Curator, row leader, joking around with Paco, winning corporate rewards she knew were meaningless. It was surprisingly easy to imagine. I considered the possibility that Mr. Bray's threats were unwarranted, and that the process would be seamless, and everyone would get what they wanted. I turned this possibility over in my mind and filed it away, awaiting the information my next encounter would bring.

⧗

The car dropped me off at the parking lot outside the park ranger kiosk by the sign denoting the entrance to the state park. I walked down a straight away, the border sloping over the limestone hills on my left, behind a dense patch of myriad plant species all vying for space, half-hewn paths lost nearly at the trailhead. The main road curved toward the border with another heading west toward the small dunes that sloped down to the beach. I followed the curve, where Gabe had instructed me, and saw Tijuana emerge before me—the bullring that hadn't seen blood in a century and a half, the lighthouse, the canyon-carved freeway, our distant maquiladora atop the hill, overlooking the construction site. A few trees shaded an observation point near the borderline that matched the description Gabe gave me. The hills were marred with erosion, deep grooves hollowing out the slopes like cavitied teeth. I crossed the final straightaway that emptied at the bottom of the park. Helicopters circled the estuary. The warm air reflected off the sand and met the ocean breeze forming a shimmer that made downtown ephemeral. I heard the flush of a toilet somewhere below the observation deck then saw Gabe emerge from America's southernmost restroom.

"Welcome to the greatest state park in the country," he said, walking up to me. A triangle awning strung between several poles shaded a handful of concrete picnic tables and cast-iron barbeques. Two gardeners uprooted weeds along the sidewalk abutting the grass. Gabe walked with me along the knee-high adobe wall that enclosed the park, his stride slow and contemplative, leading me to a set of trees each of which had its own box amid the tilework, the shade from one overlapping with another. Gabe sat with his legs hung over the adobe's edge and I joined him. Gabe put a finger to his lips and pointed to a gray fox—or as Gabe informed me: *Urocyon cinereoargenteus*—that lay before us napping, its ash-colored fur blending with the estuary reeds.

"They eat jack rabbits." Gabe whispered. "Rats. Opossums. Voles, mice. All kinds of birds and insects and, if their territory permits it: berries, corn, assorted nuts, apples and even grass. Pretty, huh?"

He handed me the binoculars and I imitated interest, even focusing the lens for effect as the fox trotted away, its bushy tail floating above the grass line.

"Gray foxes are lucky because people find them cute, so they respect their status as an endangered species. Myself, I'm concerned for the less cute ones like the Light-footed Clapper Rails and the California Gnatcatchers—two of our endangered bird species. Good luck getting locals to organize to protect them. But if they went extinct you better believe we'd hear complaints about mosquitoes and flies. Insectivores are the unsung heroes."

"Who are they?" I said, pointing to a small group standing in the restricted part of the estuary near the river mouth.

"Researchers. They're pumping dye into the river to study how the water mixes with the coastal shelf."

At the beach, a young man stood in red water. He knelt and dipped a test tube in, examined it, and logged something on his clipboard. Surfers caught the red waves that crashed off the coast while a jet skier cruised to where the water calmed and took notes on what she saw. Gabe pulled out two granola bars from one of the myriad buttoned pockets on his park ranger uniform, handing me one, anticipating a comment I neglected to give.

"Did you notice?"

He pointed to the wrapping. I looked at the small print that read: *Sourced from 100% integrated waste.*

"They developed a wrapping that uses repurposed fiber waste to create a paper-like material. Feel it. Doesn't it feel like paper?"

It felt more like particle board.

"*That* is what our grandkids will be using for everything."

I chewed the earthen bar that was closer to mulch than food.

"Good, huh?"

"It is."

He smiled, peeling an orange so that it formed a tight spiral as he turned it in his hand and I thought of how to keep the conversation going while I watched a duck near the edge of the river submerge his head only, wondering if he did that just to avoid talking to the other ducks.

"Are you fond of Yosemite?" I said, sharing the only park-related comment I could think of. Gabe stopped the perfect spiral of his orange peel.

"Yosemite is not the ideal. Especially for us State Parkers. The folks who work there don't care much about insectivores of any kind, in fact, they're much more concerned with escorting VIPs to scenic views. And when they're not doing that, they just tell tourists what to do while they strut around, ya know, soaking up the attention and all that. The park is popular, yes, but it has nothing to do with the National Parkers who work it—it has to do with how the valley looks at sunrise. Places like that are self-evidently beautiful, any random person can show up and gape. Not me. I'm a State Park Ranger, through and through. We point out the beauty to our visitors *because* it may not be self-evident to them. The estuary is only beautiful to those who know how to look."

He interpreted my lack of enthusiasm as a sign of being unimpressed, which I was, but only because I found nearly everyone, when conscious, unimpressive. My line of work, when combined with sleep deprivation, made "unimpressed" my homeostasis. Gabe changed tack and went straight to the topic at hand—the topic that prompted this meeting.

"So—Nora. Tough cookie huh?" Gabe said.

"One could say that."

"So what's your plan?"

"I don't know. I thought you might help me."

He smiled, looking at the mangled cacti arranged like a human pyramid frozen mid-tumble. Bunnies the same color as coyotes sat poised on a dirt path before scattering into the brush at the sound of a helicopter landing at the Navy base adjacent the estuary.

"Approaching Nora is like ... let me explain it this way: did you know we have jaguars that are native to North America?"

"No."

"It's true." He paused for effect. "Jaguars used to migrate from central Mexico all the way up to Tucson but over the years the migration patterns changed with the border and the ones who ventured the farthest north during the migratory season got stranded. Only the males ventured that far north so they couldn't breed and when the final few up there died they were extinct in the United States. Or at least they were until I came upon one when I was stationed in the Sonoran Desert." He bit into an orange slice and wiped the juice from his chin. "I remember the jaguar reclining in an evergreen oak like it was the most natural thing in the world. And ya know what, Sol? When I was face-to-face with this jaguar I felt fear, but it was like the fear you feel while staring at the Milky Way long enough to feel small in the good way. Nora's like that to other people when they first get to know her."

The last time I saw the Milky Way was on a documentary—but I did not tell him that.

"The jaguar and I held each other's eyes long enough that we didn't fear one another. I don't know how to explain it. Have you ever felt that, Sol? Standing in front of something you're afraid of long enough not to be afraid of it?"

"Yes."

"Then maybe you'll be able to be with my sister."

He placed the orange peel on the adobe wall we sat on and looked at the estuary. Palm trees sprung up wherever there were houses. Mountains to the east rose above the city, the nearer ones dark blue, the further ones getting lighter and lighter until dissolving into the sky altogether. I said something out loud that I thought I said only in my mind.

"San Diego looks small from here."

"Yeah."

Below us, a coyote pawed the estuary reeds, stretching its long legs with a yawn. We walked through the park as the gardeners packed their equipment into a truck and waved to Gabe, who addressed them by name. Then we walked down to the lower portion of the park, past a gully with two concrete gutters feeding into a drain and stopped short on the path as a rattlesnake wound across it, Gabe grasping my arm to ensure I did not disturb it. The snake followed the tire-line a bike had made until it disappeared into the undergrowth and we continued along the path and arrived at Gabe's truck. A horse trailer passed us, its dust trail dampened by the evening moisture. The sun had dipped below the horizon, leaving an indigo sky in its wake. Gabe turned the headlights on to reveal a man and a woman hiding in the creosote bushes. Neither moved.

Gabe silenced his walkie-talkie and sent a text from his phone. The figures stayed prostrate in the glow of the headlights. Strips of carpet or some sort of canvas covered the bottom of their shoes. Gabe whispered a prayer under his breath. A couple minutes passed with the only sound being the crickets waking until we heard the rev of an ATV headed for us. The two sprinted and Gabe turned the ignition and maneuvered the truck to keep the headlights on the runners as the ATV sped by. I watched a plastic water bottle swing from one of runners like a ball rubberbanded to a paddleboard. They reached the extent of our headlights and were replaced by the red taillights of the ATV moving up and down in the darkness. Gabe drove toward the exit of the park and came upon the ATV parked to the side of the dirt road where the runners sat with their heads down. The officer gave a thumbs-up as we passed. The short drive back to the center was accompanied by Christian music that played over the stereo. He parked beside a truck that sat charging and neither of us moved for a few moments.

"I could've watched those two laying there like that for hours—like I watched that jaguar." He looked to me for some sort of response I didn't give, before relaxing his gaze on some unseen place in the dark while he recalled something impossible to describe. "I was drawn to that jaguar somehow, or maybe we were drawn to each other, because he stayed too, all stretched out in the tree, staring back at me with his tail swishing. I remember I sat on a rock and turned my hands up like this"—his palms opened skyward—"like a monk. And as the sun went down, the sky turned red and gold and pink and I often think of me sitting on a rock with that jaguar in the evergreen oak, each able to kill the other but not needing to because we'd sat long enough to realize it." He paused, looking into the dark as if his next words could be found there. "With Nora, you have to sit with her long enough for her to know she can trust you not to hurt her. Ya know?"

"I can do that."

He opened the door and got out of the truck and I did the same. The sky was darker now, turning the distinct features of Gabe into a vague shape before me.

"Nora mentioned your church could possibly use some fundraising assistance as well."

Gabe leaned against the gate of his truck, the motion-sensing light of the visitor center clicking on to reveal his familiar smile.

"We only take money from our members, Sol, but if you wanna come by to see what we're about, you are always welcome."

He thanked me for coming and went inside for some end-of-shift paperwork. I was alone in the gravel parking lot when a car rolled in and idled before me. The driver door opened upon my approach and I got in. Before I could say an address, it moved forward with no destination showing on the dashboard.

Dirt and sand from the eroded hills limned the road, confusing the sensors that controlled the tires, and edging the car toward the middle of the road until it straddled the dividing line. A fence topped with razor wire and hazard signs perched in a clearing beside a path that switchbacked toward the border. The road bent around stables where horses slept and a ranch house that was missing half a roof, then continued past pine and eucalyptus whose thin leaves swayed with the air displaced from the car. I felt like I was in a movie, like this was happening to someone else and I was just watching, detached, ambivalent as to whatever waited at the end of the road for the character within the car.

Another curve then a long bridge leading north, away from the park. The double-yellow line wiggled on the uneven asphalt as if finger-painted. The only sounds were the road underneath and the helicopters overhead.

The estuary on my left formed a dark plain for miles, the only light coming from downtown, a thirty-minute drive away. The vegetation crept over the sides of the bridge, swiping the door of the car every few seconds until the bridge ended and stop signs signaled the unofficial end of the state park and the beginning of the city.

The car's engine cut while I waited at a red light. I thought about the old woman, Uno, who'd been bundled up and loaded onto a truck; how routinely Paco handled it, like he was moving a sack of concrete. The stoplight turned green and the car took a right, through a neighborhood with streetlights and multi-story houses, porch-lit flags; places where kids ran inside to warm meals in two-parent homes.

I thought about my brother, Jordan, how he would take his plate upstairs with him in high school and work on whatever it was he was always working on. I didn't envy him back then, per se, but missed his presence at the table, not because we were especially close but because he would absorb so much attention, diverting it from me. His routine was very precise. He would nod to my mother, then to my father, pick up his plate, thank them both and tell them he had to finish working. He would pour himself a glass of sparkling water and return upstairs with his plate and his glass and my father's gaze would follow him, as if on a swivel. If I'd timed these occurrences, the difference between each time would be negligible. It began as an anomaly, my mother insisting *Just this once* while my brother would smile and continue doing what he'd already decided he was going to do. She said *Just this once* enough times for it to be embarrassing for everybody, so she stopped saying it and would, instead, reference how this must be a particularly challenging school project for him or that becoming valedictorian is not without sacrifice, saying these things aloud as if to attract a response but her tone and affectation indicated she wanted none. My father said little.

I followed his example two years later—almost. I was salutatorian of my class, but didn't get accepted into MIT like he did, so I settled for Emerson across the river. I didn't see him often in college even though it was a ten-minute drive between the schools. I could see his dorm building from the park where I used to eat lunch. The extent of our communication was a one-line commentary on Formula 1 race day. It was his one non-work-related hobby/interest. He used to allocate 95 minutes on Sundays to watch the race and I would watch as well, mostly because I knew he was. Afterward, I would text him something like *The rain made the track too slick for Mercedes today* and he'd respond always with something contrary, like *It wasn't the track, it was the pit stop timing,* but had I mentioned the pit stop timing, he would've blamed it on the rain. That's just how he was—always taking the alternative viewpoint.

Our favorite team was Mercedes, his favorite driver was a dominant four-time champion named Jäger, my favorite driver was his teammate, Tremblay. Mercedes had a hierarchy on their team—Jäger was the clear number one, Tremblay, the number two. His job was helping Jäger win and the team accumulate as many points as possible. If the responsibility for not finishing a race could be laid on the driver, my brother always would. "Unacceptable" was his favorite word. He used to end arguments by saying *Well that is unacceptable* and that would be the end of the conversation. I understood his fascination with the sport immediately. In Formula 1, winning and losing can be decided by one-tenth of a second and a driver can die if he makes a mistake at the wrong time and place. These stakes appealed to Jordan.

It took someone of his intensity to not only invent a new technology—a software that captures, visualizes, and tabulates memories—but then to seek investors and create a start-up firm to pioneer this new field. He chose San Diego. I joined him later on because he asked me to.

I don't know why these things came to my mind as the car charged through yellow lights then slowed to a crawl once the residential streets gave way to multistoried businesses. A road crew jackhammered the street before me, causing a queue I was at the end of. To my right, a building towered above, several windows lit, allowing me to see accountants crunching numbers on one floor, customer service personnel on another. In the far window on the third floor, I watched a woman changing from high heels to sneakers, placing the heels in a special bag she carried for just such a purpose. In another window, a man played Five Finger Fillet but instead of a knife thrusting through the open spaces of his fingers it was the edge of his phone. A few times he caught a knuckle or a fingernail and would shake it off before starting a new round. In another, the desk was situated against the window, with a petit woman curled under like an embryo.

I tried rolling down the window, but it was stuck. I flicked the door lock and it snapped back. I pressed the main console, but no light came. The LED sign that measured the queue waiting for the road construction turned to SLOW and the car rolled forward and I watched the heavy machines carve up the asphalt, moving in a coordinated, fluid movement. It became hard to breathe—the A/C was off and the windows remained sealed. The further the car took me the less I focused on my surroundings and more on how to crack the window. Sweat percolated on my forehead. The glove compartment was locked; the car was empty, devoid of anything that might be useful.

I thought about calling 9-1-1 but didn't know what I'd tell them, so I didn't. Instead, I felt the rubber lining of the window, running my finger along the arc of it until I found a patch missing, allowing me to feel the window's edge pressed against the doorframe. I remember having seen someone manage lowering a window by moving it sideways back and forth to gain at least a half-inch of space. I took off my belt and tried wedging the buckle between the seal of the doorframe and the window but my fingers kept slipping on the surface of the buckle. Even though that small patch of rubber was missing on the inside, the window edge still slotted into the metal lining of the doorframe, making my idea futile unless I just broke the window. I considered how to do this—by wrapping my belt around my knuckles and punching the glass? Or pressing both feet against the window and kicking it out? I pictured Jordan watching me and shaking his head at how inept I was at solving a problem that probably had a simple solution.

I tried the window button once more, pressing it gently at first, then applying more and more pressure. I heard a click—but the window didn't move. I jammed my thumb on the button as hard as I could until I heard another click—but still no movement. I looked out the window and realized I couldn't see anything—the car had stopped moving. I pressed my fingers against the rubber lining again and could feel a little air coming through. Sweat now dripped from my forehead as I kept pressing the down button again and again, getting a fraction of a centimeter with each press until the fractions accreted to a quarter-inch of space between the edge of the glass and the top of the doorframe which allowed cool air in. I wiped the sweat on my sleeve and took deep breaths until my heartrate lowered a little. I breathed in through my nose, smelling rubber and dank air, like a forgotten basement. I heard a machine whirring and my heartrate quickened. The darkness was total. Another machine revved behind me, another above.

Then—water. Streaming in from each passenger window in the quarter-inch of space I had made which, somehow, was the same on both sides. The car was a two-passenger with no trunk, so the water started pooling at my feet in the span of thirty seconds. The sprayer wetted the windshield and rubber whipped against the windows, one of the strands hitting my nose. I wiped soap from my eyes and tried the door handle—locked. The sprayer was even with the gap in the window so water streamed-in unabated. The water level was at my knees now. I thrashed in the front seat, getting my feet off the floorboard and onto the window to try to kick it out but my foot was caught in the seatbelt and by the time I untangled it the rubber brush was lathering soap across the window—putting pressure on the outside that matched the force of my foot on the inside. The water rose. I could not see six inches in front of me. I tore at the laces of my shoes until I got both off. I shoved my hands into my shoes and tried to force the window down without slicing my fingers, but it would not move. I kicked against the windows, trying to keep my chin above the water while I lay horizontal. Nothing. I hyperventilated. I knew that even if I was able to get my shoes back on, I wouldn't have enough force to break a window if I was moving through water. I pulled out my phone to try to call 9-1-1—the water was at my chin and rising.

Then—the spouts stopped, the dryers turned on. There was still six inches of space between the roof of the car and the water level and in this space I breathed. The dryers took a full minute to dry the car, which finally moved out of the car wash and into the parking lot where a hundred other cars were assembled in perfect rows. My eyes took a few seconds to adjust to the light that came from the streetlamps. As the car recharged over the next hour, I was able to drain some of the water by cupping handfuls and splashing them through the window, watching the liquid seep down in an avalanche of suds. My ears were ringing when I took a break, the water finally below my shoulders.

A child walked up to an empty charging pad with a fistful of batteries. He placed each on the center of the pad, one at a time, watching the battery ignite in a green flame for an instant. He was crouched in a ball, his eyes peering out over the tops of his knees. He wore glow-in-the-dark shoes and didn't look afraid at all when he noticed me in the car. I didn't call for help and he didn't offer any. Instead, we both watched the last of his batteries burst into a green flame. I tried the door handle again and when I looked back up, he was gone, leaving the five batteries in a charred pile on the platform.

When the car completed charging, it rolled off the pad and onto the road, coasting at a calm 45 mph until it came to a stoplight beside a police car. I banged on the window until the officer turned to me and shined her flashlight into the car to see it was mostly underwater. She re-routed my car from the console of hers and we both pulled to the shoulder and she asked me what happened, interrupting to respond to the radio on her shoulder strap. She called the fire department who sent a truck and two men pried the door open. The water spilled across the shoulder, wetting the asphalt. The police officer took my information and an account of everything I could remember as the firemen gave me a towel and blanket and the officer decommissioned the car, tagged it, then asked where I'd like to be dropped off. She pointed to the symbol of an hourglass that was branded on the steering wheel, something I hadn't noticed until then, and asked me if I recognized it, and I said I did not even though I did. I gave her an address several blocks from mine and she drove me toward downtown.

I had finally regained my normal breathing pattern in the

passenger seat of the cop car and the police officer was kind enough not to make small talk. The only thing I could think about was my company's symbol on the steering wheel. Had they sent the car to me on purpose? If so, what was the purpose?

We reached the destination and I thanked the policewoman and waited until her cruiser was out of sight then walked three blocks in wet shoes before getting on my street. I passed the house with the pine tree and the one with the swimming pool encased in blue glass before coming to the lobby door, swiping my card, and taking the elevator. I hung my suit coat, linen shirt, and pants on wooden hangers in the closet and angled my shoes against the closet wall to dry out, making a mental note to get new laces. Finally, I lay down and slept for the first time in a week.

⧗

My evening walks through the gardens of Balboa Park lengthened to avoid going home, my shoe bottoms turning a dark purple from all the fallen figs I stepped on from the tree by the dog park. I would pass by Mr. Bray's apartment and watch him from across the street as he sat by his window and looked nowhere. When I got home, I lay awake with my back on the floor, staring up, breathing through my nose. Every so often, something roiled within my chest, something deep and restless, and whenever that happened I would go to the nearest golf course with a shovel and pound divots in as many putting greens as possible until I heard a security guard.

When I could not sleep but did not go out, I would play a livestream of scuba divers exploring some part of the world—the wall across from my projector turning the color of ocean water, the shade varying depending on the depth: clear, green, aqua, blue, navy blue, black. There was never any sound to the videos so all I would hear was the freeway traffic and the sound of planes passing overhead. I alternated theories about the memory Nora had that Mr. Bray wanted so desperately which helped distract me from thinking about what happened to my brother or what just happened to me.

CREATIVE: [0001] <UNO>
TRANSCRIPT BY: [SOLOMON ANDREWS]
DIALOGUE APPROXIMATED

START.....................................
The sky is pink and blue. Dusk. Neighbors filter into the room. People stand or kneel beside the coffin and say a prayer. I look at the baby's still hands that someone had folded over each other.
I get in the back seat of a car beside two kids. They look away from me, scared by my eyes of different colors. I watch a small girl fall asleep on the shoulder of a boy.
We arrive at the cemetery. White crosses mark the graves. Voices surround us. I look at the middle of the cemetery where people are gathered around a new hole with a cross and a pile of dirt beside it, holding candles, faces aglow.
I watch the small black box lower into the grave via frayed ropes and the sky gets darker. Feels darker. An old man sits in his wheelchair, barefoot. He gets up, stands to his full height, picks up a handful of dirt, drops it in the grave. Everyone is stunned. I see the old man walking on his bare feet down the line of crosses.
END.....................................

CHAPTER 7

I thought about my brother today. Not about what happened, just about him, who he was. As I spend more time with Mr. Bray, I realize the two have certain commonalities, my brother like a younger version of him. They are adept at making it seem like the way they saw the world was the only way of seeing it. Every argument, therefore, was a war of attrition until you capitulated to their worldview. Maybe I was drawn to these temperaments.

Mr. Bray told me to meet him at a place I did not expect. The elevator doors opened onto a pool with a neoclassic design that made entering feel grand, as if each visitor should be met with an ovation. The pool overlooked the Coronado Bridge with its pinprick lights shimmering over the black water where a yacht of drunks cruised past an aircraft carrier.

I sat on a patio chair watching swimmers unzip the water before me in their respective lanes: arms chopping the surface, mouths gasping every few seconds—one attempting to butterfly on the right, the result being closer to drowning than swimming. I watched one motor down the center lane in black trunks, no goggles. He freestyled, then backstroked and I could tell, even though he was submerged and in the dark, that it was Mr. Bray. He swam with shark-like precision—hands slicing the surface at an angle, mouth emerging just enough to catch a breath while conserving energy. I kept expecting him to crawl out after each lap but instead he reversed toward the opposite wall by pushing off with his feet and starting the next stroke. Finally, after I had stopped counting, he climbed the stainless-steel ladder on the side opposite me. Water dripped in thin streams from the ringlets of his trunks as he waited for a hotel attendant who brought over towels which he took without a thank-you, batting away attempts to help. I followed him toward the deck, noting the ease of shadowing a blind man, his graceful movement in water not translating to land. We reached the ledge that overlooked the bay. Mr. Bray ran his fingers through his hair which was transitioning from gray to white, a touch of yellow in the back. Seeing him unashamedly shirtless was even more disarming than clothed. He was thick but not obese, like a koala. He glanced over his shoulder where I stood, as though he could feel my presence the way dogs can feel an earthquake before it happens.

"You are not in the appropriate attire," he said and whistled for the hotel employee. Mr. Bray whispered something to him and the man nodded and started walking toward the glass doors on the other end.

"Follow him."

I followed the hotel worker through sliding doors and down a palatial hallway until we arrived at a closet in one of the corridors. It had everything—shampoos, lotions, snacks, magazines, phone chargers, sandals, water bottles, glasses, mugs, towels, robes, and swim trunks. He lifted a pair of XXL trunks off the shelf and took a 16-ounce Diet Coke and put it to his cheek, then stuffed it in a freezer and handed me the shorts and disappeared. I found a changing room next to the sauna. I put my shirt and tie in a locker and tried on the paper-thin trunks, yanking the drawstring tight but not tight enough so that I had to use one hand to keep them from falling. Old men emerged from the sauna, pink and wrinkled, changing wordlessly into leisurewear. A former client was among them, but he did not recognize me. I didn't remember his request, but I remembered his behavior, excited by the indiscretion, a common sentiment for one's first Curation.

I passed through sliding glass doors and saw two young women standing in the shallow end near the spa so I walked down the pool's other side not because they were attractive and I was embarrassed, but because the walkway was smoother on my shoeless feet. I arrived at the spa via the circuitous route where Mr. Bray sat by himself. Stone columns encircled the spa. I sat on the chair beside the water.

"Get in."

"I'd rather not, Mr. Bray."

"I don't care."

I took a few deep breaths to calm my heartrate, images from being half-drowned in the malfunctioning car flooded my mind.

"I think I'll remain out here, Mr. Bray, I can hear everything you are saying clearly."

"Come here," he said motioning me to draw closer. I moved the chair to the edge of the spa and leaned down, close enough to notice that his breath smelled like antique silverware. The scent was familiar but recalled no memory. He clutched the back of my neck and pulled me into the spa. My arms churned the water until I came up for air a moment later, gasping.

"Calm down, darling."

My hands gripped the sides while I tried regaining my breath.

"Breathe. Put your back against the jet, it feels nice."

I did as I was told, positioning my back against the jet which funneled water into the back of my trunks, blimping them. Mr. Bray's black knuckle hairs swayed in the spa as he scrawled something in the bubbles that parted and reformed around his finger. Steam collected in beads on his nose as he sipped a Diet Coke. The young women walked over and set their robes on the floor next to the jacuzzi and inched their lithe legs into the water, but Mr. Bray told them to fuck off and they walked away cursing in Portuguese.

"Well? What do you have to say for yourself?"

"What do you mean, Mr. Bray?"

"I thought you were good at this. Now, I'm questioning my judgment."

"My specialization is in Curation not Acquisition."

"Young people love to make excuses."

"Normally when I am assigned a client, he or she is already amenable."

"So?"

"I am not adept at convincing clients to part with memories. It's not my area of expertise."

His palms made a clicking sound as they dappled the surface. We listened to the hum of the jets, the docking boats and murmurings of pool talk. The columns supported the domed roof of the spa where the steam disappeared in static dark. I pushed my finger through a cluster of bubbles that linked together to form a ring before dissipating as the jets shut off and we sat in the calm water.

"I know everything about you," he said.

I started acclimating to his no-context statements, learning to wait for the threat to emerge from the subtext.

"I don't know what you mean."

"I am the reason behind everything in your life, darling."

"I don't understand."

"Did you think I'd go into business with someone I couldn't control?"

He let out a gravelly breath through his teeth and finished his Diet Coke in one long swig and set the bottle sideways in the water so that it floated on the surface. I looked at the beachfront houses of Coronado that glowed lantern-like in the darkness and thought about when he and I first met six months ago, an encounter that lingered in my memory like an earthquake. The water's meniscus formed a collar around his neck. The Diet Coke bottle was half-full of spa water and the label turned over a few times as the jets turned back on and the steam rose all around us, catching the light.

"I know you can't sleep and wander around at night. You don't even know why you do this, but you know it is better than staying inside and not sleeping. You're trying to escape something you can't escape and you don't even realize it." He paused and leaned back against the spa's edge. "Do you know what you are looking for, Sol?"

"No, Mr. Bray, I do not."

"A pilgrimage. Some place to purge all your grief. You'll never do this of course, but it's what you need, what you're looking for. We, Catholics, understand this. We understand why we needed physical things to galvanize belief. Without the physical, you're toast, done, obliviated. Forgotten. How many generations have we had that were so desperate to fall for something? To worship something? The Catholics were brilliant because we said, *here, this,* worship *this* right *now*. And pay for the privilege," he stopped, eyes narrowing. "What? You think this is horse shit?"

I did not respond.

"My mother was cured of stage four pancreatic cancer—think that's horse shit?" he said. "I was a boy at the time. Doctors gave her days to live. *Days*. My father was blubbering, all beside himself, inconsolable and useless. Family came by and said the ineffectual things people say in those situations and the more pragmatic ones discussed Hospice and her will and the like. Everyone was preparing for the inevitable. I stopped going to school just to stay beside her all day and all night, reading to her from her large-print bible because she wouldn't listen to anything else. As her days were waning, a priest came to the oncology ward to visit my mother. I can picture him in my mind. Short with a round face and a beard. He greeted us with a dignity that can't be faked. Treated my mother with respect and she listened to him. You could tell from being in the room that she revered this man. He asked her if she'd be interested in going to the countryside to have mass. She said yes. All I remember of the mass was the sound of the choir in the vaulted ceilings of this rural church. My mother insisted on standing and sitting at the appointed times with the others, so I helped her up and down. She weighed 95 pounds at that point. I held her steady as she walked down the aisle to receive Eucharist. As the priest was blessing the elements and dropping the wafer into my mother's mouth, he asked for Divine Presence. I remember those words even though I thought the whole thing was horse shit. *Divine Presence. Divine Presence. Divine Presence.* Those words echoed in my mind the rest of the day and as my mother slept that night back at the hospital. The next day – she was fully healed. You can call that horse shit but it's true."

His face relaxed in the way of someone just having made amends. There was no clear option for response, so I did not. I looked at the bay filling with fog. He moved and settled beside me in the spa and put his wet hand out, grasping the air until it made contact with my cheek.

"Get Nora hooked up and I will tell you exactly what to do."

"What memory are you seeking?"

"One that will heal me."

I was used to clients being highly motivated or even obsessed. This was different. Water collected along my forehead and I did not know whether it was perspiration or condensation. Mr. Bray's eyes were staring at a fixed place in the white foam of the water as if entranced. I stood up and put one foot on the ledge.

"Did I say you could leave? We're not done with our meeting."

I remained with one foot in the water and one on the lip of the spa and waited. He let the silence saturate for a few seconds before getting out of the spa and drying himself and I stood dripping on the concrete beside him, staring at the Diet Coke bottle ebbing in the water as another two people got in and unfurled an inflatable beer pong. The hotel attendant led Mr. Bray toward the changing room and he called over his shoulder, informing me that the hotel attendant would return my clothes to me beside the pool and that I would be meeting him outside of the lobby in twenty minutes. I listened to his footfalls smack the granite. The hotel attendant returned with my clothes without a word. I found a bathroom, changed, then took the elevator to the first floor and walked across the marble entrance and through the doors, watching the cars queue up in the roundabout. After another ten minutes, I heard a walking stick rolling along the sidewalk until it stopped even with me. Neither of us spoke as we got into one of the luxury cars. Mr. Bray said his address and the car merged with traffic beyond the hotel entrance. Four stoplights in front of us changed color in unison.

"Describe to me what you see outside right now."

I looked out my window and did not see anything I would have deemed worthy of describing but went ahead anyway.

"I see a man and a woman on a balcony drinking boxed wine above a 7-11. A family of tourists all wearing the same sandals. A tow-truck with its emergency lights on. We are passing under the 5-freeway now and there are expensive cars parked along the sides. People sleeping on the sidewalk beside them. The divider line on the road is fading. An average-sized man getting out of a car and entering the first floor of an average-sized apartment. Palm tree branches all over the ground."

"Jesus, this sounds dull." He turned to me. "That is your view of the world? That is what you see?"

"Yes, Mr. Bray."

"You still have your sight, but you might as well not. You don't see anything. Do you realize that?"

"I suppose not, Mr. Bray."

The car slowed to a stop outside of his apartment and we got out, his plastic cane snapping together to its five-foot length and tapping in front of him until we came upon the courtyard door which opened at his touch. He set the cane in the corner at the bottom of the stairwell beside a side table with empty vases and I followed him up, going slow, his legs trembling at the last few steps. He collected himself at the top.

"It's time you helped me with the map."

He walked to the door with the hourglass knob, opened it, and disappeared inside. I followed him, a tremor running through my body I could not account for. The room had a familiar smell of incense. It was small, could barely fit two cubicles, and empty except for a wheelchair, a desk with a computer and a printer of some sort. The wall to our left was covered in white sheets of paper and to our right —blank except for a city map fitted neatly on a corkboard. The dots of Braille were at each juncture where words would have been—denoting what I assume were streets, neighborhoods, freeways, landmarks—the borders of each raised off the surface. Mr. Bray handed me a box of pins. He picked up three papers, each typed solely in Braille, holding them up.

"These are from a previous session."

He did not elaborate, instead, he slid his finger across the first line of the first page, lips mouthing the words that only he could read. Every few sentences, he would call out a geographical feature, such as "West" or "Northwest" or "beach" and I was not sure if I was supposed to be writing these features down or remembering them. My concern about his mental acuity started growing, the idea that he was psychologically unstable occurring to me for the first time as he paused and ran his hand along the map, index finger following the raised ridge of a freeway that deployed from the center.

"It's on flat land … off the Segunda …" he said, finger tracing the Braille, "near a Walmart…" his fingers continued along the road as he mumbled something unintelligible. He pointed to the part he was referring to, then felt the nearest clump of dots that, I assume, corresponded to the name of some landmark.

"Put a pin there."

I picked up one of the pins and stuck it through the map and into the corkboard. The city looked like a puzzle piece—the straight line on top demarcating the border line. Freeways branched from the center like blood vessels. Mr. Bray discarded the first paper and picked up the next and kept reading with his finger running along each line from left to right, punctuated every few lines with a spoken direction or landmark—*south, golf course, hill, Highway 1.* His finger traced the map over different places, circling streets and falling along one road or another, course-correcting based on the document's information. He stopped at a place to the south, near the edge of the city.

"Put a pin there."

I did so and he dropped the paper he had been reading from to the floor and continued to the third but only made it four lines in before folding it in his hands.

"Have you heard the story of the Tower of Babel?"

"No, Mr. Bray."

"It's in the bible. You have heard of the bible?"

"Yes."

"Why don't you go grab a copy? I have one in the bookcase in the living room."

I walked out to the main room to the bookcase and thumbed past copy after copy of books I had never heard of until I came to a thick weather-beaten bible with gold lettering across the spine and front. In the bottom-right corner on the cover was a name too faded to discern, engraved in cursive. I brought it back to the room with the map and gave it Mr. Bray. He took the cover in his hands, feeling the gold lettering, his thumb resting on the name in the corner a long time before handing it back, his lips trembling for a moment until he cleared his throat and the man I'd known up until that point returned.

"Open to Genesis 11 and start reading from the first verse." I looked at the table of contents and found Genesis then flipped to the correct page. It was large print, the paper's edges tinted red. I started reading.

"'The whole earth was of one language, and of one speech. And it came to pass, as they journeyed from the east, that they found a plain in the land of Shinar; and they dwelt there. And they said one to another, Go to, let us make brick, and burn them thoroughly. And they had brick for stone, and slime had they for mortar. And they said, Go to, let us build us a city and a tower, whose top may reach unto heaven; and let us make us a name, lest we be scattered abroad upon the face of the whole earth. And the Lord came down to see the city and the tower, which the children of men built. And the Lord said, Behold, the people is one, and they have all one language; and this they begin to do: and now nothing will be restrained from them, which they have imagined to do. Go to, let us go down, and there confound their language, that they may not understand one another's speech. So the Lord scattered them abroad from thence upon the face of all the earth: and they left off to build the city. Therefore is the name of it called Babel; because the Lord did there confound the language of all the earth: and from thence did the Lord scatter them abroad upon the face of all the earth'."

Mr. Bray had sat down in the seat at the desk, his hands clasped atop his stomach in a post-feast way.

"I love that story. Do you know why, darling?"

"I do not, Mr. Bray."

"Were you not raised religious?"

"I was not."

"Well, I was. Went to Catholic school all the way through to college. If I thought my mother was religious before her healing, it was nothing like after. It broke her heart when I drew ridicule from my teachers..." he trailed off, chuckling. "The thing I questioned was why God, if He's *really God*, would incessantly need all this praise and adoration from mankind while insisting we're reliant on *Him*. Yet I don't see the Hebrew people ever ask God to exalt *them*. To exalt their power, their might, their strength." He waited for me to respond, but I did not. "People don't think about these things anymore. Maybe never did. But I do and here's what I've concluded, here is the truth, darling, pay attention: the message of the Tower of Babel is that it is not man that fears God, but it is *God* that fears *man*. God is constantly appeasing us just enough so we won't rebel and eradicate Him altogether. The Catholic Church is such a brilliant institution because it uses peoples' fear of God for governance, setting up an entire bureaucracy that is the peoples' only access point to God. A global organization comprised of participants who cannot question the will of the Pope because it is also the will of God. Brilliant move. And yet the Catholic Church has just one flaw—it does not realize that God fears man. Eliminate that flaw and the institution attains perfection."

I waited for him to continue and he did.

"God appeases us just enough so that we won't create another Tower of Babel and get the job done this time. No one else seems to know this. Well, darling, it's time we finished building. We're close now, aren't we? You've been an instrumental bricklayer, Sol, and I'm grateful. That's why you're here tonight—I wanted to thank you and tell you to continue forward. One more memory."

He pinched my cheek and held it a few seconds then let go and walked out of the room and took his corner beside a half-empty bottle of Diet Coke that had sat out all day.

"I want confirmation that she will agree to a Curation very soon. I'm running out of time. If you do not deliver on this, Sol, you can expect more car rides like the one you just had. Understand?"

The memory of the water filling up the car came to me. How did he know about that?

I backed toward the staircase and descended, exiting to the courtyard then the street. A car sidled up to the sidewalk, and my stomach turned over, and I broke into a run. I ran down Sixth Avenue until it leveled out and I keeled over and vomited on a fire hydrant. I could feel someone watching me, but I didn't search for them, I just walked home slowly, trying to regain my composure.

I never noticed how dark the city can get at that time of night, how scant the streetlights are on Sixth once you get away from the park. I passed the theatre that was hosting an opera and watched the people exit, people dressed up in their best approximation of glamor, pretending that San Diego was New York for a night. I pictured my brother among these, comfortable in that setting, and I wanted to leave but there was nowhere to go.

⧗

On Saturday morning, people formed a line on the sidewalk that wrapped around the church in the middle of City Heights, a part of San Diego intuitively avoided by most. It was overcast but still 75 degrees, the humidity making my clothes stick. My blood felt thick, as if someone had hooked me up to an IV of liquid sausage. The cars accumulated on the intersection where the church sat.

One of the church workers gave me a raffle ticket—telling me to give it to the person at the front entrance which was somewhere near where the line bent toward. Translators from the church monitored the line and intervened when an argument broke out in Vietnamese or Somali. Across the street, a camo-jacketed man towered above a volunteer, berating him for some unintelligible offense as the volunteer handed him individual food items—an apple, a cantaloupe, two boxes of trail mix, a loaf of whole wheat bread—which the man placed in his bag. After the exchange of items ceased, the camoed man landed an emphatic *FUCK YOU!* before leaning against a nearby tree and settling in for a nap. The volunteer crossed the street and shrugged at me before joining the line facilitators. I watched Gabe emerge from the back of a U-Haul in the parking lot that was surrounded with a steel fence that had to be open and closed by hand.

"Welcome, brother!" Gabe said, calling to me from the back of the truck.

He wore a clerical collar and the black shirt I had only seen in movies, coupled with faded Levi's. Behind him were loaves of white bread, cartons of canned fruits, sealed birthday cakes with frosting untouched, and produce that had at one time been fresh—all stacked floor to ceiling. He started filling my arms with heads of lettuce and celery and grapefruits. He knelt and scooped up a pile of bread and hopped out and I followed him toward the courtyard where volunteers in plastic gloves stood next to folding tables. The space was tennis court-sized, with high walls and movable furniture. The courtyard had a drain in the center and a dark splotch on the concrete that looked like blood but probably wasn't.

"I've been thinking about our conversation the other day at the park and you made me realize something. It's so simple, I'm sure you already thought of it.

"In order to show Nora that there's nothing to fear about you—and that you aren't afraid of her—the best thing to do is what you're doing right now with me. Participate in something she enjoys."

"What does she enjoy?"

"I mean where do I start? She loves softball, bowling, coffee, card tricks, music, dancing, libraries, skating, you name it. Anything where she's in motion. Have you seen the skatepark yet? The one at the library?"

He glanced up from the loaves of bread he was arranging on the table. I shook my head.

"You should start there. To win the heart of a skater girl is to understand the world of skate."

I thought about Gabe's affection for cliché and decided to build off this, delivering a cliché in a tongue-in-cheek way while also acquiring vital information and moving the conversation forward.

"Do you both have a father I need to impress or exes I should be aware of?"

Gabe shrugged with a smile that contained layers.

"We're orphans. Nora and me aren't blood-related. We just showed up at this orphanage around the same time and stuck together."

"Ah, I see."

"As for the exes—all the previous guys she dated couldn't keep up with her after a few dates, so nothing's really panned out there. Don't let that scare you off though. You've already lasted longer than most."

We moved on to setting up other stations—placing small containers of broccoli and pears on one before moving to another where we dumped mangoes into boxes that had formerly held bananas. I was told four different times not to give any of the banana boxes away—that several people would ask for them, but

I was not to give them away under any circumstances. Gabe told me later that due to their durability—they were triple-layered in an impressively difficult-to-break waxed cardboard—the grocery stores that donated the unsold food required the return of the boxes the food was delivered in. Banana boxes were offered in lieu of cash in some parts of the city where bartering was still viable.

"How 'bout you? Any maniacal exes?" he said, washing watermelons under a spigot and handing them to me to place on a crate. I didn't know how to answer his question because I couldn't recall why I broke up with my last girlfriend but remember it was amicable and that I didn't miss her.

"None worth mentioning."

"No vengeful lovers? Really? You seem like the type!"

Gabe laughed and escorted me to the next table with a gentle hand on my shoulder. We stacked more canned food pyramidically. At the back of the courtyard were the flour products—the bread, cakes, Danishes, and so on. Gabe instructed each of the teenagers working at the tables on how much to allocate each person before turning to me to finish his thought.

"If you show up to the library's skate park and spend a couple hours there, you'll learn a lot. Go down there and you'll know what I mean. Nora will appreciate it hugely, but she'll never tell you that. That's not her style. She has her own little ways of showing appreciation."

He picked up a rotted zucchini off the ground and disposed it in the nearest trashcan, then clapped his hands as he looked out at the volunteers. He had already broken into a sweat, his dampened forehead made enormous by a receding hairline. He had a music conductor's energy as he pointed at places to put extra cans, or where to return the broom to, or where to put the broken-down cardboard.

There was a nervous tension developing in the line outside that

Gabe attuned himself to, periodically dropping by the line to quell an agitator or instruct someone that yes, in fact, she had been cutting and needed to go to the back of the line—the raffle ticket always being the smoking gun. He disappeared for ten minutes and returned with two cups of coffee from a diner across the street. I tasted the coffee and told him it was good but needed to cool down a bit while he went to pry a child off the fence and I dumped the coffee in the planter of a dying Ficus.

The line's chatter sounded like any until you stood close enough to hear the conversations. I heard Spanish, French, Portuguese, and Mandarin during a single pass down the sidewalk. Everyone had something with wheels—a pushcart, bike with basket, rolling backpack, suitcase, stroller, cooler. Each held their raffle like it was the last plane ticket out of a warzone. Some had kids asleep in the stroller or holding their hand or running through the line playing tag. Gabe ruffled the hair of the ones he knew in-between breaking up fights in the line. The large brass bell in the church steeple rung and the line hushed, looking up at it, assuming their respective places amid a few elbows. Gabe took me by the shoulder and led me to a meeting hall with a few scattered chairs and the refuse of long-ago church activities: butcher paper signs beside boxes of tissues and little crackers encased in plastic bins. A mother approached Gabe to explain how her 12-year-old son suffered from night terrors and he prayed with her in a language that was unidentifiable. They hugged and she left.

"You ready?" he said.

"I believe so."

"You don't sound all that ready," he chuckled and gave me the three-second shoulder massage that people like Gabe think alleviates tension instead of heightening it. We watched the volunteers assemble at each of the food stations through the tinted windows of the meeting hall, there being a palpable camaraderie among them shown by the five-second dance-offs they did to kill time.

"Where would you like me to stand?"

"You mean to *serve*," he smiled. "How about you take the ... let's see ... how about the bread table? Sound good?"

"Okay."

He escorted me out to the table stacked chest-high with bags of twelve-slice loaves and introduced me to a girl named Brianna who was clearly there because she was forced to be and I was relieved at the near certainty that she would not be compelled to converse. A laminated sign taped to the front of the table informed the beneficiaries only one item was permitted at this table. The front entrance doors were opened, the distribution beginning with a man in an XL Pittsburgh Steelers jersey and his partner beside him who'd whisper things into his ear and avoid eye contact. They made their way down to us and he picked up two loaves, pointing a thumb at the woman without elaborating.

Gabe twisted the pumps of hand sanitizer bottles until they popped up. Each table had one and most went unused. He would periodically take a dollop in his palm and wipe his hands together, using it probably the same number of times as everyone else combined. At one point, someone bumped a table where a teenager had stacked grapefruits and about twenty hit the ground, unharmed except for the dirt they collected on the rinds. Gabe gathered each one and placed them on a separate table, then unfurled disinfectant wipes from a secret stash in his pocket and cleaned the dirt off with the concentration of a surgeon before carefully placing them back on the corresponding fruit table and reprimanding the kid in a way that sounded more like encouragement than admonishment.

The people passed through, filling their carts/bags/ strollers/

buckets with whatever the grocery conglomerates didn't want. Most were polite. Some had a look like they wanted to explain why they were there but couldn't, so they settled for a *Thank you* that sounded more like *I'm better than this.* A squat woman picked up two cakes—a lemon meringue and a chocolate—at the station before mine and the high schooler tried to explain to her that only one was allowed, his hand holding the other side of the second cake she had chosen. The woman said, *No, two fine,* trying to pry it from the kid's hands but the kid dug his heels in saying *No … solo uno,* biding just enough time for Gabe to come over and address her by name—the cake still suspended over the table. At this point, the line had stalled, a couple Cambodian men giving voice to the general annoyance of all the others with words I did not understand yet could infer. Gabe did not budge.

"Only one dessert, Anamaria, only one."

"I got kids, birthday, come on Gabriel."

Gabe gave one of those diffusing-the-situation smiles.

"Anamaria, it's been one of your kids' birthdays each month for the past year."

"Nephews and nieces, claro?"

"Lo siento, hermana."

She said fine, then yanked the meringue so that the plastic cover tore off the top and frosting went all over the high schooler and Gabe. The former started tearing up with rage, but Gabe just laughed and took the kid by the shoulders, wiping the frosting off of the adolescent's cheek and asking for someone to bring a damp cloth for each of their shirts. The teenager settled down and Gabe walked over to me, shaking his head.

"She's going through something, huh?"

"Perhaps."

"She is," he said, nodding.

"I didn't know you were a minister."

"This old thing?" he said, tugging at his clerical collar with one finger. "This is just so they know who to talk to when there's a problem."

He stood with me at the bread station while I handed out loaves to those passing through, the ones he knew—which were most—received some part of him, be it a hug or kiss or fist-bump or handshake or a *How is your family?*, all amounting to an extroversion I didn't expect from a man who spent his days monitoring California Gnatcatchers. Perhaps he saved up his extroverted time to expend in one three-hour period among people that no one else cared about. I started handing out the loaves without looking at the recipient, thinking I might expedite the line that way. I did this for the next eight or so people until someone stopped at my station and did not move forward. He had long dark hair that collected around his shoulders. I recognized him as the one who'd always driven Uno to the maquiladora month after month. Gabe watched without saying anything, even as murmurs turned into outright demands, in various languages, to move on. The young man handed me the loaf back.

"Where is she?" he said, barely above a whisper. He unfolded a piece of paper to reveal a photo of an old woman, happier than I'd ever seen her. I shook my head, pretending not to know that he was talking about Uno, our most reliable Creative, who'd been stuffed into a bag and loaded on a truck that drove somewhere east of Tijuana.

"Where *is* she?" A bit louder this time.

Gabe looked to me for an explanation, but I said nothing. The calls for the young man to move forward went unheeded. He was as tall as me—one of the few.

"Where. Is. She?"

"I don't know who you are talking about."

I expected him to set something aflame. Instead, he kept eye contact and removed a hair trimmer from his pocket and proceeded to buzz his hair in smooth lines—all of us standing motionless while he did. The trimmer's sound echoed in the courtyard. When he finished, he shook off his shoes and walked away barefoot as Gabe stared at the circle the long strands of hair made on the ground. He remembered where he was after a moment and waved the next people through, while he found a broom and began sweeping it up. I put on my sunglasses and rolled up my sleeves, as if doing any small action would break the spell.

Gabe tried retaining the joviality he'd begun with, but it felt forced and he gave up, resorting to quiet encouragement to those he felt still needed it. We made eye contact a few times and he gave the muted smile people give in public places. After the last person collected from each station, I waited in the parking lot by the U-Haul as Gabe bid farewell to the high schoolers, signing off on some community service form they each had. He locked the back door, then lumbered across the parking lot and unlocked the U-Haul and we got in. He drove us just past the gate, then parked momentarily while he threaded the padlock around the fence and through the chain. He scrambled the gold digits of the lock, pushed it in three times and tugged it several more times to make sure it had locked. He took the driver's seat, his hand on the keys in the ignition.

"What was that all about?" he said.

"I don't know."

He looked at me, eyebrows arched.

"Who was he referring to?"

"Not sure."

Gabe pulled onto the street and we waited at the stoplight. The air conditioning pumped through the vents on the highest setting, chilling me even though it was summer temperature outside. I considered explanations for why Uno's relative asked me where she was, inventing different possibilities for who the young man and "she" were, wondering if I could construe a coherent enough narrative to sustain follow-up questions. Each of the explanations were either too cliché ("she" being my ex-girlfriend and the young man being her new lover) or too obscure ("she" being a client protected under some sort of client confidentiality). I decided to stay quiet and allow time to dissipate the event.

We pulled into the loading dock of a Vons parking lot where Gabe greeted the store manager. We unloaded a few dozen banana boxes onto a pallet then drove the U-Haul to where the compost/recycle/general waste dumpsters sat. I half-expected Gabe to lecture about how proud he was of this branch composting etc., etc., but he just dropped the cantaloupe and lettuce in, pausing only to instruct me to undo the plastic wrapping of the bread before tossing in. We offloaded the cardboard and hoisted the garbage bags into the general waste bin.

"Where do you want me to drop you?"

"Anywhere is fine."

"Alright."

He turned on the radio and browsed a few channels before turning it off a few minutes later, drumming his fingers along the steering wheel at stoplights. He pulled into a dead-end street by the entrance to the 805. I opened the door of the truck to get out.

"Thanks," he said offering his hand. I nodded and shook his hand. The orange turn signal of the truck clicked on as he pulled back onto the street and I thought about the young man and the circle of hair he left and knew that Gabe was thinking about him too.

CHAPTER 8

When I called Nora to meet up, she exhaled for twenty seconds, before telling me that yes, she would show me how my $27,000 had been spent if I stopped by that evening. I got in a car while it was still light out, the fog shifting from Chula Vista to Tijuana like a husband lending his spouse a coat. The library stood at the edge of a park, where intergenerational chess-playing transpired at stone tables with chessboards etched into the surfaces. Deciduous trees shaded a gazebo behind the library where a crooner song a ballad with a mic carrying his voice over recorded instrumentation. He tipped his fedora when a tourist dropped coins in his little collection bucket. Two septuagenarians danced together, revolving in a small circle, the man spinning the woman, their gaze releasing from each other for only that instant. I heard a flirtatious whistling-sound behind me and paid no attention then looked back when it returned. Nora was leaning against the rail, looking at me through her sunglasses.

She held the back door open for me and led the way to the skate park via the main floor of the library, where the librarian, Carlos, was switching off lights and kicking kids out of the movie theater room. Carlos tossed the keys to Nora and she unlocked a side door. Something in the aisle caught her eye. A kid, not more than eight-years-old, held a book so close to his face that he didn't notice Nora, who snuck around him on all fours. When she was even with his ear, she yelled *WHAT ARE YOU READING?*—

startling the kid who threw the book across the carpet in response. Nora kicked him out and picked up the book—something called *El Toque de su Piel*—and placed it back on the shelf with a chuckle. The side door led out to a concrete area where a few skaters rolled around a pit. I saw a metal rail about knee-high next to some cones that huddled around a patch of jackhammered cement.

"Voilà."

"Impressive."

Her eyes narrowed, suspecting my unsarcastic response was in fact sarcastic.

"Okay dude, it's a work-in-progress, I'll grant you that, but it's gonna be dope."

She did a roll call, pointing to a kid wearing Dickies two sizes too big and said his name was Manuel, then to another kid in a beanie whose name was Joaquín, then to a third named Maricela, who wore kneepads and a helmet. None of them gave so much as a nod.

"Is that a swimming pool?" I said, pointing to the pit.

"It *was*. Now it's the main attraction of Tijuana's first Skate Park Library or—dare I say—Baja's first Skate Park Library."

We circled the perimeter, Nora pointing to each feature of the place, using skate jargon to describe a piece of concrete that had been molded into a 45-degree ramp next to a slope with a rail bisecting the center. One of the skaters played music from outdoor speakers which made Nora pause her description of what she called a *Banked Extension*.

"Manuel, what is this? House music? How many times have I told you that when I'm here, you have two options: Wu Tang or Wu Tang?"

The kid looked at the phone which controlled the music and a few seconds later, the music changed to a song with a slower tempo and more drug references.

"THANK YOU," Nora said and resumed the tour.

A few older kids showed up and greeted her with a fist-bump and casually dropped into the former swimming pool. I watched one launch out of the bowl and kick his left foot out, grabbing the front of his board while a friend captured it on video.

"That's called a 'Madonna'," she said, unpocketing a pack of sunflower seeds, and dumping a few in her mouth, then puffing her cheeks to launch the seeds at the passing skaters. When she'd hit the target, the victim would feel the back of his neck in confusion before continuing on, living with the mystery of what the sudden wetness was. Nora wrapped her hands around the soles of her Converse as we listened to the beehive hum from the skateboards reverberate throughout the park. The sky turned cathedral blue. Kids ate Cheetos on the pool's ledge. Nora launched another seed and hit another skater.

"I'm tired," she said, sitting down and leaning back, her palms flat against the ground. "On Wednesdays, I make seventy-five bucks an hour to walk a couple dogs and hang out with entitled little shits. But it's not their fault. Or so I tell myself. It's a good gig except when the dad starts flirting or the mom solicits therapy. The ones with older kids all have the exact same epiphany when they realize buying their kid a Benz when they turned sixteen probably wasn't the best thing for them. It's like, yeah, *no shit.*"

Maricela, the lone female skater, stood at the edge of the pool with her pink board hinged on the lip, watching the boys cross in spaghetti patterns below. A kid her age ollied and slipped on a rail to her right, hitting his knee and cursing in a pubescent pitch. Her legs shook as she backed away. We watched her idle a few minutes until she picked up her board again and looked over the edge like it was a Nietzschean abyss. A few of the others skated by, teasing as they went. She bit her lip, little arms shaking, everyone turning to watch her as she backed away. The boys laughed.

"Fuck this," Nora said.

She got up and joined the girl beside the pool's edge. Nora bent to eye-level, brushing aside the girl's bangs so they could see each other clearly, then took her by the shoulders and spoke in a quiet, assertive tone—the girl punctuating each statement from Nora with a nod. Nora slapped her helmet and backpedaled a few paces as the girl approached once more. The whole group watched.

She took a deep breath, looked at Nora, closed her eyes, stepped on her board—and dropped down. She made it halfway down the slope before the board slipped out from under her and she fell hands-first. Before she could think about whether or not to burst into tears, Nora cheered—arms raised—and shot the boys a look that demanded solidarity, at which point they joined her cheering. Maricela looked up, showing her scuffed hands and smiled. She tried climbing back up with her board but only made it partway, so Nora along with the kid in the beanie came over and hauled her out. She ran to the same spot and dropped in again, falling once more, but this time on her kneepads, cushioning the slide to the bottom and Nora pumped the air, watching the girl try again and again and falling again and again until she could drop-in without slipping from her board. A couple floodlights turned on as Nora came back to me.

"Part of your 27 grand paid to have that pool buffed so Maricela didn't shred her palms just now."

We watched the boys welcome Maricela into their group with fist-bumps. Nora nodded toward a kid eating Cheetos and reading *Harry Potter* below the floodlight, the pages balancing on his knees.

"In order for the privilege to skate here, every kid has to have a library card and at least one book checked out. When we first started doing this, the kids thought they could blow it off. Yet after a few times of getting denied access, they got the message and began checking out books. I monitor the records every day to make sure they have a book in the pipeline. Manuel is on the fourth *Harry Potter*. Alejandro in the yellow over there is reading a book about cars. Joaquín—in the beanie—reads romance novels but that's our secret. And Maricela, she reads mostly sci-fi. Stuff like *Ender's Game*."

There was that summertime energy of after-hours mingling—the kind that beer ads commodify—the kind that doesn't really exist but somehow did then and there. Everyone wore t-shirts and time was immaterial. The kids laughed at inside jokes. Breathing felt easier. I watched a small child roll marbles along the ground, every marble containing all he needed to hold his attention, his little hands palming the ground as he searched for each one. The sunset was colored like a pilot light. As time passed, the color dissolved into a softness like the underbelly of something. Nora turned the floodlights off and on, signaling the end of the session, and all the kids protested but knew negotiation was futile, so they picked up their boards and their books and went out the door on the side entrance. Maricela stayed behind to tell Nora about how fast her heart was beating before she dropped in that first time and how she felt like crying when she fell and how it felt a little less scary the next time she tried it and even less the next and the next and I saw Nora smile and it reminded me of something familiar that I can't remember. After they all left, Nora told me to follow her into the library. She led me into the movie room then disappeared and reemerged with a bottle of tequila.

"Do you like tequila? Actually—who cares if you like it, someone needs to drink this with me and you are the only one here."

She picked up a remote and clicked a button that turned the projector on. She selected the *Films in English* category, then *Classic Films*, and filtered through the movies. The covers of the films she clicked through were old, with paintings of melodramatic lovers and vengeful gunmen and things we'd grown out of. I recognized certain names yet could not put faces to them, like Clark Gable, Humphrey Bogart, Marlon Brando, Robert De Niro. She settled on one called *Cool Hand Luke*.

The film begins with the protagonist being arrested for cutting the tops off parking meters. He's thrown in a country prison somewhere in the south then shown, three scenes later, "winning" a fight by losing—the barrel-chested boxer pummeling him over and over until finally tiring of the protagonist staggering back up, the spectators and dominant boxer's willingness dissipating before the titular character's. Later, Luke eats fifty eggs to win a bet, and Nora turned to me and said she'd tried that but only got to five. I watched her watch the film. She leaned forward as a prison guard locked away Luke in solitary confinement, the former apologizing to the latter by saying he was only doing his job and the latter informing the former that his rationale doesn't make it right, the camera capturing both grimaces.

Nora made fun of the overacting yet mouthed every word of a banjo ballad sung in the following scene after Luke hears of his mother's death. Throughout, Nora poured more tequila into each of our small paper cups, the kind that accompany water coolers.

"Do you think there're certain people who are so undeniably attractive they transcend the homosexual/heterosexual divide? Take *Cool Hand Luke*—it's painfully clear in this movie that half the dudes in the prison would fuck him if they could. And that's not because he's Prison Hot, he's just Hot Hot. He transcends the homosexual/heterosexual divide. What do you think?"

"I've never thought about it."

She turned toward me, narrowing her eyes. "What *do* you think about?"

"Work."

"What the fuck is your work? I never got a clear answer."

"Simply put—I observe memories."

I spun the timer on my watch, a habit I'd acquired when nervous. It was a little wheel that circled the hour hands. Whenever I was on a job, I set this timer to remind me not to go over the allotted sixty minutes, even though the digital clock was always working atop the computer screen. I liked to manipulate the watch as a way of occupying my hands with some type of movement—each twist making a little, satisfying click.

"What do you mean *observe memories*? How's that a job?"

"I told you about it once before," I said, tasting the tequila and letting the burn of it provide me a reason to pause and allow her to retrace our previous conversations.

"I vaguely recall something like that, but I thought you were joking. I think I'm getting drunk enough to listen to something insufferably boring so go ahead and explain."

She refilled our tequila cups. Luke escaped the prison and was on the run, enlisting the help of two African-American boys who brought him an axe which he used to cut the chains on his feet.

"My firm acquired this technology that enables the review of peoples' memories."

"What?"

"The software populates human memories into a timeline that we can observe."

"I guess I'm actually not drunk enough yet," she said, taking another shot. "Continue."

"We acquire certain desirable memories that our clients purchase to embed as their own."

"Okay, dude, I'll follow you down your weird fuckin' rabbit hole," she said, taking yet another shot. "So the memories they purchase become their own memories?"

"Yes."

"You *surgically* put them in peoples' brains?"

"Not surgically. The embedding is seamless, our process requires no invasive surgery."

She laughed and slid lower in her theater seat, trying to drink without using her hands by biting the edge of the cup and tilting it up with her lip. She succeeded, then set the cup beside the bottle.

"I know this is a strange joke you dreamed up for some untold reason, but I'll continue to play along just to see how far you're willing to take this," she said. "So, let's see ... what questions would I ask if this were real ... I got one—how does someone know if their memories are valuable to another person? Why would my memories be valuable to someone else?"

"That's my job—to determine which memories are valuable and recover them for our clients. Your memory would become his after the transfer process. Hypothetically."

"What do clients usually find valuable? Girl-on-girl?"

"It varies depending on the client."

"People just pay for memories they don't want to go out and get themselves? What pussies."

"They want to live many lives. Why live one life when you could live a thousand?"

Nora shook her head, refilling her tequila. The colors from the movie played across her face in the otherwise unlit room.

"Why do you do this? Speaking hypothetically, of course, because there's no way this shit is real."

"I know it is difficult to grasp. To answer your question, I do this job because it is well-compensated."

"Are you not well-compensated?"

"Not as much as I could be."

She laughed for some unknown reason then took several seconds to regain her composure. She splayed her elbows, taking both armrests.

"For money, then?"

"Yes."

She repeated the word *money* several times in a hushed tone as if doing so would help her understand the idea behind it.

"Have you seen memories you weren't supposed to see?"

"Yes."

"Like you were supposed to be looking for something, but you couldn't help looking at another thing?"

"Yes."

She bit the edge of the cup, rotating it in her mouth until the whole rim was covered in teeth marks. Nora seemed to be among the cohort of people who could smell dishonesty, so I decided that any question Nora asked, I would answer honestly, reasoning either she would forget it anyway due to her current level of intoxication or it would lead to a deeper level of trust between us.

The final scene of the film transpired, Luke was trapped in a church asking why he's been forsaken. His pursuers arrive and he mocks them. They respond with a bullet through the church window. The barrel-chested boxer from the earlier scene tries choking out the gunman whose glasses are knocked off and crushed by the tires of the police car/death carriage that transports Luke's body. The credits rolled, eventually returning to the blue menu screen.

"What did you see that you weren't supposed to see?" Nora asked.

"Virgin sex."

"How'd you know that's what it was?"

"The Creative—the person selling memories—was Mormon."

"How do you know?"

"I saw his undershirt all Mormons wear."

She drummed her lips with her fingers, pantomiming thought.

"Were they bad at it?"

I shrugged.

"What does"—she shrugged—"mean?"

"When they undressed each other, the husband cried and the wife cried, and they whispered all the things they loved about each other. And when he moved to insert himself, something was not working and she said that was fine and they embraced the rest of the night and he was so relieved."

"How do you know he was relieved?"

"I could feel it."

"How?"

"The same way you feel anything."

She poured the last of the tequila from the bottle into her paper cup and drank it, twisting her head after it had gone down. She looked at me, eyes half-mast.

"I don't believe you. I think you made all this shit up."

"Would you like me to show you?"

"How?"

"You could come to my work and I could show you."

She squinted at the blue screen, confused where the movie had gone. She got up out of her seat, steadied herself, straightening her shoulders.

"Hypothetically ... if this technology actually exists and you can show it to me—well then I'd want you to show it to me through you."

"What do you mean exactly?"

"I mean I want one of your memories, homeboy."

"My memories are not very interesting."

"I'll be the judge of that."

"You cannot remove a memory of mine without replacing it with one of yours."

This was not true.

"What do you mean?"

"Even our clients trade a memory for the one they purchase. A memory they do not care for."

"So, if I want one of your memories, you need one of mine to make it work?"

"That's correct."

"Deal." She spit on her hand and held it out to shake and I lamented this attribute of hers but performed the ritual all the same. "Time to get me home. And no funny business."

I pointed my phone's flashlight at the ground to see the path to the door, Nora holding onto my shoulder to steady herself. The door locked behind us and we crossed the main library room to the front door; the books on the dark shelves felt like sleeping friends. Once outside, Nora pulled the front door shut, then scraped her keys across the doorframe, trying to fit the correct one into the keyhole. I called a car and got in despite my body reacting with a rise in blood pressure. She told the car her address and we glided away from the curb, my stomach turning as it has in each car ride since that one night. Nora's eyes started to close then catch and close again like a garage door with something in its way. The yellow moon shone above the mountains and over the hillside the city was built on. The car took precise turns and made subtle maneuvers around potholes until it slowed to a stop outside Nora's apartment where it waited patiently at the curb for us to disembark. I allowed Nora to sleep another two minutes, if only to delay the solo ride back home without a second person to intervene in the scenario of another malfunction. Finally, I decided to wake her but didn't know the appropriate method, so I remained still instead. The fluorescent ceiling lights eventually came on and woke her. She searched for the door handle with a sleepy hand but could not find it, so I got out and opened the door for her. She got out and walked to her front door, opened it, and went inside, turning one lamp on. Through her front window, I watched her collapse on the couch, her face between the pillow and armrest, then I buckled my seatbelt and took the car home.

CHAPTER 9

No better city exists for Curation than Tijuana, with its abundance of foreclosed properties that made private Curation readily accessible. These were the industrial taupe buildings with tinted windows—the Brutalist buildings people think of when they think of prison or asylums. The company owned one of these; I identified it by the sign of an hourglass that stood near the entrance. I texted Nora the address and set everything up with Paco's help, whom I paid $500/hour freelance. I was unsure if she was more curious about the technology or my memories. I could not imagine why it would be the latter but, then again, most of Nora's behavior fell into the category of unimaginability.

"Sup boss."

Paco arrived wearing a Hawaiian shirt, his sandals clacking the floor and kicking bits of drywall as he walked. I opened a stainless-steel locker and removed a plastic container while Paco wheeled out the generator. We unboxed the modem, router, gel pads and laptop, taking a few minutes to unwrap the wires and plug in the necessary items. Paco was ten years older than me, so working with this equipment came naturally, he not having to second-guess which cord corresponded to which opening as he plugged the router in and unscrewed the cap to fill the generator with diesel, cranking the starter rope until it purred. He unfolded two chairs and spaced them a shoulders' distance apart then unclasped the legs of a square table where he set the laptop.

"What is this place, boss?"

"A former branch."

"That's why we still got all this shit here?"

"We still use it occasionally."

This was true. Sometimes, a client insisted on complete discretion and we offered this space—only me, the client and 2,000 square feet of empty space. My brother had liked contingency locations and this one was his favorite.

Paco handed me a hard drive. I connected the hard drive to the old Dell laptop with scratches all over the bottom. Paco handed me the end of a cord and I plugged it into the computer's port and the gel pads ignited. He peeled back the edge of the paper that covered the pads and felt the adhesive with his finger and gave me a thumbs-up and pressed the paper back on.

"When's the Creative getting here?" Paco asked.

"I'm the Creative."

He cocked his head with concern—trying to downplay the awkwardness he felt—then decided to ask the question on his mind.

"You low on cash, boss?"

"It would take a long time to explain."

He nodded. "So—you want me to stay or … ?"

I examined the setup—router and modem were blinking, gel pads glowing, their wires neatly coiled between the chairs. I clicked the trackpad of the laptop and it awoke, showing the dull blue background. I opened the Curation software to see the familiar message—*AWAITING INPUT.*

"A new Curator is coming here to train momentarily—do you remember the basics?"

"Yeah 'course."

"When she gets here, you will put me under then teach her the process and help her curate one memory. Show her how to toggle back to early memories. This part is important—ensure she only browses memories made *before* this year. And when she selects a memory to curate, facilitate the transfer. I'm not concerned whether the transfer completes or not, but she needs to think it does. Do you understand, Paco?"

"Yeah, boss, no problem."

"Again—do not show her this year. End the session after 45 minutes—okay?"

"You got it, boss. When she gets here, put you under, show her the ropes, nothing from this year, end it after 45."

"And do not talk to her about our line of work or anything personal, Paco."

"Alright, alright, no problem."

We heard footsteps in the stairwell and watched the doorway as Nora appeared. She looked around at the exposed ceiling, the broken glass and gravel on the floor, some paint buckets discarded near a ladder, a few wires hanging down.

"So … this is where you live? I was expecting something a little more, I don't know, upscale but I guess this 'Rubble Chic' design has its own appeal."

"Nora, this is Paco, he is an experienced practitioner who will be helping you today."

Paco smiled.

"Wow—I thought I knew something about going to great lengths for a joke, but this is next level—hiring a dude to pose as a colleague, finding a vacant, sketchy place downtown. My one critique would be the lack of a receptionist, that would've been a nice touch." She sat in the chair and looked up at us. "All in all, though, well done."

"Paco will show you how to examine, and select, the memories while I am unconscious. My only request is that you avoid memories of my brother."

At this point, I knew Nora well enough to know she would take the bait, spending the majority of her time browsing memories of my brother—which would illuminate next to nothing about me—and pass over recent events. She peered at us, crossing her arms.

"Wait—you're serious about all this? You can really look through memories?"

"Yes."

"And this guy's gonna show me how to look through yours, one of which I get to choose?"

"Yes."

She stared at me directly, unblinking.

"You? Mr. One-Word-Answer is going to let me dig through your most intimate, embarrassing, and personal memories? And that's all possible, huh? You are going to let me do that today and this guy is going to show me how?"

"Yes."

"Alright then, sure. If you're right, I'll see shit you would never imagine telling anybody—you're okay with that?"

"I trust you."

She nodded like she was talking to a schizophrenic. Paco stood in his Hawaiian shirt with his hands clasped in front of him trying to look patient but failing. I reminded Paco to end the session after 45 minutes and he nodded and removed the paper linings from the gel pads and placed them on my head as I relaxed in the chair. The last thing I remember was Nora's expression which I could only describe as concerned—the kind of look she would've never let me see under normal circumstances.

⌛

When I had regained consciousness, Nora was beside me. I told Paco that he could leave and he winked for some reason. She grabbed my arm and hoisted me out of the chair and informed me that we were going to the beach. We took the stairs down to the street where a vendor had laid out dozens of pairs of leather huaraches, sandals, and other slip-ons. Our car pulled up beside the shoe vendor and Nora got in and I noticed her jeans, not because they were form-fitting and well-shaped, but because her back pocket held the hard drive with my memory. Nora had spent enough time with me to know that silence did not bother me at all and I think she had grown accustomed to it not bothering her. I watched a motorcyclist with a sidecar weave between the cars headed to Playas de Tijuana. The man driving was helmetless, the wind ballooning his yellow tank-top behind him as he looked from the road to the sidecar's occupant—a boy with a helmet and goggles—each as happy as the other. The car carried us over the hill and down, past a Walmart, taking a wide street that ended beside a basketball court with net-less orange hoops. We crossed the street and took a footpath made of stone steps down to the boardwalk, covering our eyes from the sand kicked up by the breeze.

The vendors sold ice cream from a cart and Nora bought strawberry on a cone, the flavor bearing thick chunks of fruit. Every inch of Playas de Tijuana that could be given color was—murals were painted across the stairs, each individual step being a panel. The manhole covers were painted with smiling suns. Every tone was the deepest essence of that color—the hue you would find in a Crayon box. One house was built at the boardwalk's end, unattached to anything, a garden out front. Its burnt orange color invited the eye. A couple drank wine on the balcony. The man held the woman in his arms in an affectionate way, the kind of posture that lets the person know you are not going anywhere. They looked out on the Coronado Islands that were blips on an otherwise flat horizon.

Nora turned from the house and walked north, kicking a wad

of tinfoil up the boardwalk a few feet each time, scuffing her red Converse against the wood. She walked slow, swaying, as if her ice cream was a half-drunk vodka bottle, before settling on a bench. I sat beside her. Foot traffic passed behind. We watched a family tiptoeing around the tide water that crashed on the sand, seeing how close they could get to it then backpedaling to avoid the next wave that washed higher up the beach. Nora licked the last of the ice cream and tossed the cone in the garbage beside us and wiped her hands on my suit coat.

"Do you always dress like you're about to meet the president?"

I looked at the smudges on the sleeve of my coat and didn't respond.

"You need to chill out, dude," she said, pinching my shirt so that it untucked from my belt.

"There."

Two kids climbed to the roof of the lifeguard hut that stood above the rocks too big to hold in one hand. Their view was not much different, of course, but held that strange satisfaction derived from being on the roof of something. The sun dissolved near them, turning the sky pastel blue and pink.

"I think I know a lot better now why you are the way you are. After the memory thing."

An emaciated man walked on the beach in front of us, shirtless, yanking the reins of a blue horse that trailed behind him. His pants were cuffed above his ankles. We watched the horse's musculature amble across the sand, its saddleless body the color of the waves emptying near its feet. The man cursed, shouting every word at the ground. The horse kicked up wet sand with every footfall, not increasing its pace despite the emaciated man's constant tug, and neither of us said anything as they passed from view, swallowed by darkness and distance.

"I always catch myself doing this," she said, glancing at me.

"Thinking people are simpler than they really are."

The ice cream vendor was making his way toward us again, this time selling horchata and hot cocoa. Nora bought both and sipped from each, warming both her hands simultaneously.

"When you were a kid, what did you want to be when you grew up?" Nora said.

"A Formula 1 driver."

"Why?"

I thought about this for a moment, twisting my watch. Under normal circumstances, I would have just answered yes.

"Because my brother wanted to be a Formula 1 driver."

"That's it? Because *he* wanted to be that?"

"Yes."

She looked at me as if to respond, but did not, and kept drinking her cocoa. She seemed different somehow, like something she'd seen in me changed something in her. I wondered if my memory induced her pity that manifested in congeniality or, perhaps, I'd potentially succeeded in gaining her trust.

"That's no way to live, Sol."

"Is there another way?"

I asked this question reflexively—it released from my lips before I could change the subject and end this topic.

"Yeah there's another way. It's called carving out your own fuckin' path. Finding what brings *you* life, what gives *you* energy, what animates *you* to do something. No one can do that for you. You can't just take someone else's interests thinking it will bring you the same gratification."

"That was the only choice in my family."

"Why?"

"Because, in my family, you only captured someone's attention if you achieved something, usually something difficult. My father is a lawyer and he'd discuss winning these technical lawsuits over family dinner. My mother is an executive communications director for a pharmaceutical company and would try to outdo my father by describing her presentations to the board. Meanwhile, my brother would sit quietly until they turned their attention to him and he'd share about how he recommended to the principal of his junior high a new school bus schedule that streamlined offloading time. Then they'd turn to me and I'd have nothing. When that happens every week for a couple years, you start trailing after your brother, just to keep up, just to tread water. So when my parents asked him when he was nine-years-old what he wanted to be when he grew up, and he said a Formula 1 driver, I said the same."

She sipped her cocoa and watched a metal detectorist comb the sand, his headlamp searching the ground like a tiny UFO. We watched the lighted spot on the ground moving a few inches south with each step. Something soothed me about the idea of a person retracing your footfalls, looking for something valuable you'd dropped. Maybe the detectorists and I shared the same preoccupation.

"What do you think they find?" Nora said.

"Nothing valuable."

"Why do it then?"

"Habit."

I meant that perhaps the detectorist, as a boy, shared that activity with his father and detectoring was the only time they spent together. What if the only time he saw his father smile was when they found something—a necklace, a ring, a pair of sunglasses—and he kept roaming the same beach looking not for the thing itself but reenacting the times he connected with his father, who is gone, in the only spot possible to do so? That was what I wanted to say.

"That memory thing was fuckin' wild," she said, scuffing her shoes on the ground. "Just to see someone's whole life unfiltered like that ... like I saw a bunch of the moments you remember, all the little memories that make up your life, and realized I may as well be looking at my memories. We experience all the same shit."

"Which memory did you choose?"

"You're going to be the one transferring it, right? You can see it then."

She sat cross-legged on the bench, her change in posture foreshadowing the change in conversation.

"Why does no one know about this technology?"

"We've been profiled in tech magazines before. I am not sure why word hasn't spread."

But I knew exactly why. We had only been profiled once and the distribution of the magazine was tiny and Headquarters quickly reversed this decision after it came out, not wanting to risk the scrutiny of greater exposure. A reporter from *The Economist* had seen that original piece and wanted to follow-up but was ignored in the form of unreturned emails and zero leaks and no interview prospects.

"How did you even get into doing this work?"

"My brother recruited me."

"So many of your memories were of him."

Bonfires ignited below us with groups huddled around, their faces reflecting the warmth they felt transfer from the fire to their fingers.

"Were you close with him?"

"He wasn't someone you got 'close' to."

I looked for ways to redirect the conversation. I thought about complimenting her choice of clothing, but it was clear she had not put any effort into choosing her hoodie and jeans and the compliment would be taken as ridicule or a diversion, so I remained silent.

"Why don't you ever elaborate? Like, I have to *force* you to give more than a one-sentence response to any of my questions."

I paused a moment, debating on whether or not to say the thing I was thinking of saying.

"Before this job, I realized that every conversation I had eventually led to the same conclusion—without fail. Each discussion had an entropic force, driving it down toward that single conclusion so I stopped talking altogether to save the trouble."

"What conclusion?"

"That we're all alone."

"What do you mean?"

"I mean that you can try to understand who I am and what I've been through based on what I describe to you or maybe even by seeing my actual memories, but even this will fall short of you truly knowing me. There will always be something entirely inaccessible. There will be a point where you can no longer relate."

She didn't respond for a couple minutes and we listened to the waves crash the shore. A few stars gathered above us. The wind made her shiver. She looked over at me a few times but said nothing, as if she were editing a sentence in her head she had thought was the final draft but revealed itself to be still unpolished when it reached her lips. Her long hair fell across her shoulder, obscuring her face some.

"That's the stupidest fuckin' thing I've ever heard."

"Watching thousands of memories corroborate this idea."

"I just talked about how watching your memories made me realize I may as well have been looking at mine—that we all feel the same things. Don't you feel that when you look at other people's memories? Doesn't that make you feel less alone?"

"At the memories, yes, but those shared experiences rarely make it into conversation, leaving me and the person I may have some commonality with both feeling alone ultimately."

"But you know already! You've seen enough memories to know for a fact that whoever you're talking to feels just like you in so many ways."

"I know. But I forget."

The waves retreated further from the bonfires on the beach with each passing minute. I had never seen Nora like this—her voice trembling with a lump in her throat—a feeling I had forgotten about. I sensed Nora's judgment of my family and wanted to tell her that every individual is a complex collision of genetics, experience, and desire that cannot be encapsulated by any isolated event, any more than a single star could explain a galaxy, but I knew she would have a rebuttal that would prolong the conversation and it would take too long to explain. I never liked talking to another person outside because it was unclear how to exit the conversation—there was no door that served as a marker for where to go when you were done. Then again, I suppose talking in a room, if the room belonged to you, meant you were trapped until the other person left.

"My father is American. A gringo, no less," Nora said.

She apparently was attempting to alleviate some of what she perceived as lingering pain in me by telling me of her own painful situation. She looked to me, expecting a response which I was at a loss to give.

"I tracked him down years ago, but I never ended up talking to him."

She played with the drawstrings of her hoodie, tying them together and untying them. Nora took a deep breath and regained her composure. We watched a young woman play guitar by the bonfire, her voice drifting toward us. I understood the meaning but not the lyrics of the song and part of me wished I could have communicated with Nora that way instead of using words.

"It's times like these I wish I smoked. Just for the ritual of it, the process of removing the cigarette from the pack and putting it in my lips, cupping my hands around the lighter and striking the flint, hunching over to shield the flame from the wind."

She wrapped her fingers around an invisible pack and unsheathed an imaginary cigarette and parted her lips to hold it in place. She cupped her hand and flicked her thumb then brought it to the tip of her cigarette and puffed her cheeks a few times before relaxing her neck. She took it from her lips and let some ash fall to the ground and puffed again. She removed it from her mouth and held her hand out to me—her thumb and forefinger parted the width of a cigarette. She gave a look that said *Go on* and I reached out and took the cigarette and puffed a few times then tried to give it back, but she instructed me to take a long drag, *Like this*—she told me—then inhaled deep and exhaled. She dusted more ash on the ground and took another drag, flicking the end of cigarette after she did so.

"Why would people give up their memories?"

"For a paycheck."

"That's all? Really?"

"Is that not sufficient motivation?" I said.

"Would it be for you?"

"Depends on how much I needed a paycheck."

I placed my chin above my interwoven fingers in a posture I hoped she took as deep thinking. I knew this was the critical moment where she would decide whether or not to continue and I needed to be sufficiently convincing.

"On the occasions I've parted with memories, I was relieved. Even valuable ones, because then maybe I was helping someone else get through the day. It felt unburdening, like taking off a backpack full of lead."

This was untrue. I had parted with RAM, but mostly RAM that

was mandated to be parted with and it felt like nothing. Nora stared at me, her chin resting on her knees wrapped in her own bear hug. The wind played with a wisp of her hair and it reminded me of something. A pack of stray dogs walked together along the boardwalk, some venturing off to sniff an abandoned grocery cart in a side alley before returning to the pack. The couple in the orange house were no longer sitting on their patio, but concealed somewhere within the home, enjoying the comforts such a place offered.

"However, having a memory embedded does feel like something. Whenever a client moved away and forgot they had contracted with us—leaving behind a curated memory—or decided against Curation at the last moment, the memory would be embedded in me. After a few years of this, I don't know what was mine and what was theirs anymore."

This was actually true.

"So the memories I saw might not even be yours?" she said, her voice soft, the edge it usually carried gone.

"They are now."

"But ... they didn't, like, originate with you? You didn't have those experiences?"

"It depends on what you saw."

"Do you know which are yours?"

"Every once and awhile, I have these intimations when I am walking around and see someone doing something I could not possibly have done—like a woman at a salon getting extensions—and it jogs something that fades as soon as it arrives. Yet something does come and go. And those moments started happening ever since I started embedding."

Nora took a deep breath as a burst of spray shot out of the ocean, then a tail broke the surface. Another burst, then another—massive bodies rolling toward the end of a continental swim to these warm breeding waters. It reminded me of something I no longer had the referent for. We watched the pod of whales pass and I thought Nora was going to lean her head against my shoulder, but she did not. This memory was a good example of one strong enough to populate a screen if a Curator were to put me under. The genesis of RAM was such an inexact science. It could be because the sight of passing whales was beautiful or because Nora was Nora or because I was talking more that I usually did. I don't know.

She got up from the bench and started walking back the way we came and I followed her. She bought a sparkler from a vendor and lit it and wrote words in the air too fast to read. Kids emerged from nearby places to plead for a turn and when she gave the stick to one, he ran forward with it while the others followed, calling after him, until the spark went out and they returned, disappointed. Nora turned on her heels and bought a dozen more from the man and lit them simultaneously—bringing their violet-colored tips together under one flame—then distributed them to the kids who all bounced and ran in little circles. Nora danced, sparkler-less, in the middle of them, the twirling lines of flame like the image of car lights on a long exposure. The sparklers extinguished at the same moment—everything stood still for a split second—before a collective sigh and a rebounding energy spread through the kids once more.

We climbed the stairs that took us street-side. Nora's apartment was a few blocks from where we stood on the sidewalk wet from a recent hose-down, marking the close of day for the oceanfront restaurants.

"You're not going to walk me to my door?"

"I'm sorry?"

"It was a joke. Have a good night, dude. Keep safe. When are we doing this whole memory trade anyway?"

"Next Thursday?"

"I'm free after six. Text me the deets."

She was about to step from the sidewalk to the street when she spun to face me.

"I know you think no one gives a shit about your grieving, Sol, but I do."

She turned and walked away before I could respond. As she walked, she glanced back but it was too dark to see her face, her silhouette moving from street to sidewalk, wrapping her sweatshirt around her waist and waving as if she liked me.

⌛

CREATIVE: [03012] <NORA RINCON>
TRANSCRIPT BY: [SOLOMON ANDREWS]
DIALOGUE APPROXIMATED

START....................................

We look at three headless scarecrows that guard the opening of the drain on a north-facing slope. Each is made of branches that pierce the ground in an X-shape with clothes hung from them. Lakers jersey on the left, sweatpants with a blouse in the center, shorts and fleece on the right. They make slanted shadows on the ground. The drain is built at the base of a hill, facing a ravine, two gutters on the sides feeding water down to it.

Gabe dismantles the first one by lifting up the jersey to find the rope that ties the two branches—needling his knife underneath and sawing until the rope severs. He cuts open the clothes, disentangles them from the branches and lays the wooden spikes against the wall of the drain. He does the same with the other two scarecrows. The hill behind the drain is eroded limestone.

He lines up the branches against the drain wall

and drives his foot through each, splitting them in half and tossing the halves into the creosote. He peels the gloves off and squirts hand sanitizer in his palm. "Who made those?" I say. "People passing through," he says.

I take off my shoes and roll my jeans to the shin. Tadpoles circle my toes. "Where do you think that leads?" I say, pointing to the mouth of the drain. "Tijuana. Where do you think it leads?" "Back in time."

We sit together on the dirt slope and watch the sunlight recede from the hills, listening to birds and the hum of crickets.

A jet paves a streak of white plume across the sky, heading for the half-moon above us. The sunlight turns the plume gold and it lingers long after the jet.

Rabbits scamper across the dirt road. Gabe picks up a stick and draws in the dirt. We hear the sound of an owl close by.

I look into the ravine a long time then nestle closer to Gabe to feel safe. We hear rustling in the bushes, a flap of wings, the occasional coyote.

A red light streaks the sky, climbing high then falling in a slow arc and disappearing over the plain awash with darkness. Helicopters head toward it.

Gabe kisses the top of my head and I follow him to the quad. We drive to the parking lot of the state park and swap the quad for a truck.

A windchime made of driftwood clicks at my doorway. I grab two beers and crack both open on the edge of the tile counter.

We walk outside and I sling my arm through his. We sit on the top step of the church and look at the ocean beyond the beachside restaurants and convenience stores. We listen to the waves. The sky and water are gray-blue. We watch a buoy blink red as it bounces on the waves. I curl close to him and he puts his arm around me and provides a place for me to lean my head and I do and it feels like home like coming in from the cold like fear is gone for good. "The ocean reminds me of God," he says. "The buoy reminds me of me," I say.

We get up and take the steps to the street and turn down the boulevard, passing a gym, apartments, a yellow motel, payphones somehow still there. Construction workers wipe cement from their spades and blow cigarette smoke across the sidewalk.

We pass the merry-go-round of a street carnival and an old man is bent over a control panel with wires going everywhere, and, as I look back, the merry-go-round lights up.

Stray dogs peer at us from abandoned lots between mangled rebar.

Music drifts into the street from a restaurant's live band.

We arrive home and he cuts vegetables and adds them to the food I prepare. We eat together as families walk by outside. He leaves.

I can't sleep so I walk through an alley that leads to the beach. Low tide.

I swim in the dark, my hair sticking over my eyes and mouth. I look back to the shore and see someone I recognize so I swim back and it is my brother and I feel safe again.

I hug him and he wraps his warm coat around me and we watch fishermen in knee-high boots cast their lines into the water. They catch fish a foot in length and drop them into white buckets. The fishermen wave us over.

They show us how to prepare the fish by cutting them open and cleaning them in the salty water. We build a fire and wrap the fish in foil and set them over the flame. We drink coffee from a thermos and talk. The fishermen unwrap warm tortillas and we eat as dawn arrives.

END......................................

CHAPTER 10

Nora decided I could "use a dog." I never mentioned wanting a dog and did not know what I would "use" it for. I told her as much.

"You might change your mind when you see them," she said.

I responded with mild protestations which were cut off prematurely as she continued, saying, "Just be there in a half-hour, I texted you the address. Hanging up NOW."

The car dropped me in the parking lot of the shelter, 15 minutes from my apartment, a low-roofed building with a cartoon decal on the door. Nora was already there, playing with a Schnauzer in the fenced outdoor area that abutted the building. The Schnauzer bent to the ground while Nora held a rubber bone above her head, then swept it quickly to mouth-level with the dog who took hold of one end and tug-o-warred with Nora. She saw me and said one minute, then played with the dog another ten while I waited there behind the chain-link fence. The more I watched this particular Schnauzer, the more I could picture assimilating him into my routine, this breed having a reputation of mild-manneredness.

"Did you select him already?"

"Who, Bartleby?" Nora said, pointing to the Schnauzer. "You won't find a Schnauzer at an animal shelter—this dog belongs to the staff member."

She said this as if it were common knowledge. I walked into the lobby and was met with an empty desk where I waited another ten minutes before one of the staff, presumably Bartleby's owner, asked me to sign-in and complete paperwork.

"I'm not adopting today, just browsing."

"In order to browse you need to fill out the paperwork, sir. And please no photographs of our canine partners."

I considered responding with asking whether photography would be permitted if I got the dog to sign a release but did not. I completed the paperwork, describing my apartment, the frequency with which the "canine partner" would be taken for walks, my idea of the perfect meal (for the canine partner), the location of my preferred grooming salon, the level (1-10) of my propensity for physical affection such as "petting and embracing," and my current place of employment, all of which was the first page. I completed the five-page application and turned it into the staff member along with the clipboard. She thanked me and smiled, both forced. Nora finally emerged from some backroom and called to the staff member to send me over. I walked to where she indicated and Nora led me to the prison-like cells where the dogs dwelt.

"Shall we?"

She escorted me to the first dog—a Basset Hound missing half an ear. Nora descended into a baby-like tone that prompted suicidal ideation in me. The skin around the dog's eyes drooped a half-inch from the red sockets. His fur was white with brown and black spots and his energy level was the equivalent of a part-time security guard. He barely lifted his head toward me, knowing I wasn't the type to adopt a dog whose ratio of maintenance required versus owner pleasure was disproportionately skewed toward the former. Nora had the face of a lover when looking upon him. I started moving toward the next cage.

"Seriously?"

"I would like to peruse my other options as well."

"He's a rare find in here."

I continued on.

"Whatever."

Next was an eighty-pound Boxer. As soon as he saw us, he jumped with his paws on the cage as high as my chest. He started barking, which set off a chorus of barking until Janet, the staffer, came and cooed her way past each cell, saying something that quieted the dogs, before glaring at me as she left. The next cage held a Pug too tired to bother and the one after was empty. On the other side, we came to a Rottweiler who kept nipping his tail. Beside the Rottweiler was a chirpy Terrier that needed chloroforming. We passed an expectant Golden Retriever whose size negated apartment accommodation as well as a Chow-Chow whose eyes were barely seen in its folds of amber fur. Next was an Australian Shepherd, friendly, with a gray-black-brown coat and a white patch over one eye. He approached us, wagging his tail, and rolled over just to show us he could.

"Not that one," Janet said, her voice carrying all the way from her desk.

"But he—" Nora said.

"Nope, not happening, dear."

I looked at Nora who rolled her eyes and put a finger gun to her head and pulled the trigger. We came to the last dog in the row, a Greyhound who was also a rescue. I braced for another call from the lobby determining this one off-limits too, but none came. The dog had wheat-colored fur and brown eyes and moved his head slightly, trying to map our level of interest like a girl at a dance observing the boy she'd been told was going to ask her out. The dog was shaped like me—long and thin-limbed with a small face. Its tail began preemptively wagging as he stuck his snout through the fence to be rubbed by Nora's fingers.

"I think he likes you, dude," Nora said.

"Big dogs need space. I don't have much."

"How big is your apartment?"

"3,000 square feet."

Nora scoffed and shook her head, mumbling something about the wealthy. I couldn't understand why Nora was pushing for me to get a dog. None of our conversations over the last year even made mention of one. Rather than ask her, I tried maneuvering out of the obligation via excuses.

"Dogs require a lot of maintenance. I don't know if I am responsible enough."

"You've never been late to anything and have always picked up my calls and your clothes are never wrinkled – these are telltale signs of some Grade-A adult shit. I think you can handle a dog."

I lowered my voice, gesturing toward the front.

"Not sure I am a favorite of the staff here, so this is all a moot point."

"Janet!"

"Yes, dear?"

"How long's this Greyhound been here?"

"Oh, that one? He's been here six months."

"Any chance my associate, the tall uncoordinated one standing next to me might be able to adopt him?"

Bartleby came through a doggie door that led outside and circled our feet.

"Well, I'll have to review his application," she said. "But barring any red flags … it could be arranged."

Bartleby pawed my leg, desperate to be petted. Half the dogs seethed with jealous growling as they watched Nora pick him up. We turned back to the Greyhound in question who did not share the others' animosity for Bartleby, the two appearing to be friends or at least cordial acquaintances. I allowed myself to picture this dog lounging in the corner of the balcony or sauntering beside me en route to Balboa Park.

"I can't bring him home today. I need time to make the necessary preparations if I decide to acquire him."

"It's chill, dude. They give you sixty days after you confirm the adoption."

The Greyhound's tail wagged a little more, leavened by our continued presence in front of his cage.

"What're you gonna name him?"

"He's a former race dog?"

"Looks like it," Nora said, reading the description.

"Then, 'Jäger'. It's the name of a Formula 1 driver."

We looked down at Jäger whose mood remained even-keeled. Nora gave him one more rub on the snout before we left, dropping Bartleby at the front desk and leaving to the sound of the staff member's cooing.

"You're a dog owner!"

"Perhaps."

Nora rolled her eyes and started walking west, expressing the need to satiate her hunger. We walked to the end of the main street where the neon sign of El Cajon Boulevard demarcated the beginning of North Park. The A of the sign was unlit, creating a typo:

the

BOULEVARD

Nora craved pizza, so I followed her as she cut across the street, past an Italian restaurant to the take-away pizza place that comprised one of the stores in a tiny outlet. This particular take-away was renowned in San Diego. Loyal clientele included college students from Pacific Beach who ate this pizza after getting dumped or drunk or both in order for their stomach to resemble their emotions. It was the pizza equivalent of instant coffee. Yet Nora seemed unashamed as she ordered and paid for one large which was delivered to her surreptitiously fast. She handed them to me while she went to a liquor store two doors down and bought a pack of Modelo's.

"Those bitches carded me," Nora said, shaking her head.

"Where would you like to eat this?"

"Oh, I got a spot."

She called a car and we got in and coasted onto the 163-North briefly before taking the 8-West until it ended where the fireworks of Sea World ignited into multi-colored light, then skimmed the border of Ocean Beach and took Rosecrans, scaling a bluff at a seventy-degree angle. Another turn and the car stopped at the curb facing a dead-end street.

"Are we there?"

"Turn around, dummy."

We got out and walked down the sidewalk until the whole of San Diego spread out before us, glinting with light, like a grounded constellation. The city limned the bay, which reflected its glow on the water between the boats that blinked by. Tijuana pulsed with light to the southeast, spread across the hill that overlooked the dark estuary. We ate pizza and stared at the cities.

"What a big place," Nora said.

She spread crushed pepper on her second slice and continued looking out before us, the little docked sailboats jostling in the current made by a passing speedboat.

"Guess what I wanted to be when I grew up."

"What did you want to be?"

"You're supposed to *guess*."

"Guess an occupation?"

"Forget it." She drank her beer, the gold foil along the bottle's stem gleaming like the city lights. "I wanted to be a travel writer."

"I didn't realize that was a viable occupation."

"It's not. I just wanted someone to pay me to travel and make witty observations about other countries."

"Where would you go if you could?"

"Everywhere."

She picked up another slice of pizza, folding it like a sleeping bag and biting into one end. Airplanes queued in the sky, taking the same oblong landing route to the airport below, as if on an invisible conveyer belt. She finished her pizza and leaned back.

"Sometimes I wanna do so many things I'd need ten lifetimes to do them all and even that probably wouldn't be long enough. Then—in the same exact thought—I'm reminded of how long my own life is and the thought of getting up day after day after day depresses me."

A college couple parked behind us and talked in hushed tones. Others drove by periodically, a few parking beside the mansions that stood on every corner of that neighborhood.

"Do you feel grown up?" Nora said.

"Yes."

I understood then that her question was posed to me but was intended for her, so I reflected it.

"Do you feel grown up?"

"If being grown up means being like you, then no," she said. "You seem like one of those people who being a kid feels like a long-ago time, when, for me, seventh grade still feels recent."

She took another slice of pizza and sat cross-legged.

"Do you miss being a kid?"

"I miss not having my brother."

"What was he like?"

An unbidden memory populated my mind of seeing my brother by a little creek a short walk away from our house. I didn't recognize him at first, because I was so far away, but when I got closer, I saw that it was definitely him and that he was masturbating, but the more interesting thing, as I watched, was that he didn't seem to be masturbating *to* anything. He didn't have his phone or a photo and he wasn't closing his eyes or concentrating all that much. He washed his hands in the creek after he was done and went home, where, I assume, he continued his studies in his room. As if the release was all he needed, an impediment to get over. I realized I hadn't spoken in a full minute and Nora was still looking at me.

"He was a perfectionist."

"How so?"

"He didn't know what to do with failure of any kind."

She waited for me to elaborate until finally realizing that I was not going to, then folded the pizza boxes and grabbed the empty Modelos and walked down to the end of the sidewalk where a trashcan had been wheeled to the street for pickup. She deposited the boxes, and returned, doing high steps over the cracks of the sidewalk. I realized Nora felt most comfortable when in motion—when going from point A to point B, whether A was her apartment and B was some La Jolla home she nannied or A was merely the curb and B was the trashcan. When still, her body was merely biding time to be in motion once more, manifesting in a tapping foot, changes in posture, playing with something in her hands.

She asked if I was ready, so I called a car, the fear of riding still present but abating some because of Nora. We traced our route back, descending the steep streets to Rosecrans, then driving along the harbor, seeing at ground-level what we'd just seen at bird's-eye. A steady flow of cars took the left exits for Terminal 1 and Terminal 2 as we passed the airport, headed toward Downtown. The car turned onto Laurel and we stopped mid-way, the trolley going past on the train tracks only halting us a minute. We scaled a hill and turned on my street then got out at my apartment where Nora had insisted the Curation take place.

I opened the lobby door and pressed the button for the elevator and we waited, Nora posing in the lobby mirror as if on a runway. We arrived at my apartment and entered. As we toured each room of the apartment, she would open something that was otherwise hidden from view—in my bedroom it was the top drawer of my desk, in the bathroom it was the cabinet behind the mirror, then a canister of tea leaves in the kitchen.

"What's that?" she said, pointing to what must've looked to her like a glass microscope.

"It's a wine aerator."

"What's it do?"

"I'm not entirely sure, actually. It was my brother's."

"Do you have any wine here?"

I opened the cupboard and poured two glasses, hoping she would not ask me to use the wine aerator because I did not know how. She took her glass and wandered into the living room where she looked at the calendar on the wall.

"What's this?"

"It's a calendar with the dates and times of Formula 1 races."

"You followed the season pretty closely."

"It was my brother's."

She flipped through a few of the months looking at the annotations my brother had made before pointing to the opposite wall where a poster of a driver was framed. Jäger had the same cutting eyes my brother had.

"Is that the guy you named the greyhound after?"

"Yes."

She nodded, moving along to a record player in the corner and the collection of vinyl underneath. She took out the box and started flipping through the records, stopping at one then holding it up, an artist named Thelonious Monk whom I'd never listened to.

"Wu Tang sampled this guy. Looks like you and Wu Tang have

got similar taste. Every day brings a surprise."

"Those were my brother's as well—I can't say I've listened to them."

"These were all his?"

"I didn't discard any of his belongings after he died."

She looked back to the records, not knowing how to assimilate this new information. She picked up the Thelonious Monk album again and unsheathed the vinyl and placed it on the record player, pressing the power button and moving the needle to the first groove. A melodic piano came through over a soft snare drum. She slid open the door to the balcony and leaned her elbows on the rail, looking across at the peninsula where we had been an hour earlier. To the left, the banks and hotels with glass facades were topped with red lights that activated at night.

"What'd you do with his clothes?"

"What do you mean?"

She looked at me, glancing down at my slacks.

"You *wear* his clothes?"

I nodded.

She bit her lip and leaned against the balcony. A plane made the palm trees sway on its descent and we watched until they became still.

"Have you considered therapy, Sol?"

"For what, exactly?"

"You're joking. Wait—are you joking?"

"I'm not sure what you mean."

She shook her head and sighed.

The night grew colder with each passing hour. Nora's arms goosebumped beside me and I thought of offering her a jacket but didn't know whether she would take this as a chauvinistic gesture or think it was strange now that she knew it was my brother's. I could feel her looking at me.

"I had no idea of the extent of your grief. But seeing your memories … then learning this … it reminds me of how much you need someone to talk to."

"I'm unsure I would label it 'grief'."

"You're so lost."

We sipped the red wine and stood shoulders' distance apart, watching my neighbor make dinner for his daughter in the apartment across the street. He chopped vegetables on a cutting board while she removed a pan from a drawer and hoisted it onto the stove, just above head-height. The father slid the vegetables from the cutting board to the pan and adjusted the stove knob, holding his daughter who was holding a spatula which she used to move the vegetables around. The dining commenced on a table that only accommodated the two of them.

"I got an idea," Nora said, taking off her shoes—red Converse—and tying them together, eyeing the street near where people hopped the fence of the community garden and pillaged.

"Aren't you gonna ask what I'm plotting?" she said, bunning her hair. She took a shoestring from each shoe and tied them together.

"What are you plotting?"

"I've never done the thing where you catch a pair of shoes on an electrical line and I've always wanted to and I just thought of it, so now's the time."

I nodded, looking at my watch.

"You got somewhere to be?"

"No."

"Don't get too comfortable—you're doing it too. Take your shoes off."

I hesitated, unsure if she was serious.

"Take them *off*."

I knelt and untied my shoes, while she did little jumps like boxers do before they step into the ring. Once I had both shoes off she showed me how to triple knot them together like she had.

"We're going two for two tonight, baby."

We faced the crosshatch of wires with our podiatric ammunition, she looking to me as a golfer to a caddie.

"How far you think that is?" she said.

"Approximately 20 feet."

She felt the weight of the shoe in her hand, closing one eye to aim.

"Ready to have your bra blown off?" she said.

"Okay."

"Alright, let's *DO THIS!*"

She counted off one … two … three—swaying the shoes back on each number—and let go …

The shoes sailed through the air and roped around the wire near the transformer. There was a moment of disbelief.

"I. Just. Did. That!" she said, pumping her arms to each word. She looked back to where the shoes straddled the line cattycorner from the balcony and clapped her hands, launching into a speech thanking all her fans who supported her along the way. She settled down only after some celebratory moonwalking.

"I've wanted to do that ever since I was a little kid. I can die happy now." She leaned on the balcony once more. "Your turn."

I looked at my shoes, lamenting whatever fate awaited them. I channeled the softball pitching motion I'd honed while tossing to Gabe, practicing a few times before swinging them back and releasing them over the balcony, only to have the shoelace catch on my watch, unclasping it from my wrist and sending it the ground to shatter beside my fallen shoes. Nora laughed until she was out of breath and I left the balcony and walked to the bedroom, switched on the closet light, and selected another pair of suede loafers like the ones I'd thrown off the balcony. When I returned, Nora was in the kitchen, drinking wine from the bottle and flipping the pages of *Topography Today.*

"What the hell *is* this?" she said, holding up a feature on geomorphometrical change in Malta.

"An analysis of geomorph—"

"No, this magazine." She began reading the article. "'Terrain analysts identified hydrological shifts in topographical continuity intensifying erosion in the...'—there's no way you actually read this, no way."

"I do."

"Why?"

"It interests me."

"But this is the most boring shit I've ever read. A date with Dexter Riddlesworth would be more interesting than this."

"I'm sorry, who is that?"

"He wears *bowties.*"

She continued thumbing through the magazine while I examined her feet for several seconds. Small and smooth. Her third toe on her left foot tucked beneath her second, slightly. I looked up and she was still flicking through the magazine as she asked, casually, "So we doin' this thing or what?"

It took me a moment to recall what she was referring to.

"Yes."

I walked to the coffee table and opened my laptop. She took a seat in the Eames chair as I selected the waiver form and handed the laptop to her.

"Whenever you are ready, review the stipulations here and click the box at the bottom indicating your agreement."

Her brow furrowed looking at the 56-page document, a tiny progress bar moving on the right-hand side. She squinted at the footnotes that functioned as page breaks as well as clarifications.

"Dude, who fuckin' cares. Where is the box agreeing?"

I instructed her to scroll to the bottom and click the *I Agree* box, then to select the *Submit* button, which she did (relinquishing her memory rights as a result). I unboxed the Curation kit, plugging in all the equipment. She retrieved a set of headphones she'd been carrying in a tote, the kind that cover your whole ears, and turned them on.

"Are these going to mess with anything?"

The headphones were dark red, like week-old strawberries.

"No, they'll be fine."

She snapped her fingers, drawing my attention to the hard drive she held in her hand and passing it to me. I plugged in the hard drive that held one of my memories. It populated the screen as a folder. Nora synched her headphones with the record player, then browsed her selection, choosing one with a solid coral color and lime green text across the top, slotting it on the record player and arranging the needle. A song started playing through her headphones as I untangled the gel pads. She cleared one ear.

"Let's talk about the No-Go-Zone."

"Okay."

"It's simple—nothing from my childhood. Got it?"

"Simple enough, yes, that's perfectly fine."

"Alrighty. That's settled."

I noticed her breath quickening with the rise of her stomach, foot tapping the wood floor at 150 beats per minute. She shifted the connecting bridge of the headphones below her chin so it would not interfere with the gel pads which I tried placing but she kept insisting she place them on her own head. I handed her the corded pads, instructing where each went until all were correctly placed on her head. My finger hovered over the space bar as I waited for her confirmation so that I could engage the Curation.

"Ready?" I said.

She hesitated, biting her lip and nodding.

"Alright."

I pressed the spacebar ...

At that moment the lights shut off and the gel pads dimmed. Nora nodded off then awoke a second later.

"What happened?"

I stepped onto the balcony and noticed the entire street had no power. The blackout only extended a few blocks, its perimeter demarcated by the lighted apartments that bordered the freeway. Planes still passed overhead; the airport in the distance still glimmered.

"Power out?"

"It looks like just a few blocks," I said, detaching the gel pads from her head.

"How often does this happen up here?"

"Never."

She spun around in the chair and stood, spreading her toes in the carpet, then walked to the corner and picked up the record with the coral vinyl cover. She typed the name of the album into her phone and unplugged the headphones so it could play from the phone's speakers, turning it to its maximum volume. A song with steady percussion and electric guitar played with a halting voice that seemed to pause after every phrase and Nora danced in a similarly halting way with plenty of shoulder movement. She put a foot on the vertical sides of the chair and rode it to the ground then smoothly followed her path into the kitchen and retrieved the wine and drank straight from the bottle, offering it to me but I declined.

"Sol—live a little."

I acquiesced and when I lifted it to my lips she tapped the end, making the wine spill all over my linen button-down.

"Klutz!"

I went to the guest bathroom and dampened a hand towel with

warm water and dabbed the stain then abandoned the shirt to the hamper and returned for a second time that evening to my closet to find a suitable blue Oxford to wear. When I returned to the living room, I found Nora looking at the YouTube history on my phone. I peered over her shoulder as she scrolled through several videos about skate trick compilations, an explanatory video about the Dewey Decimal System. She scrolled further. A music reviewer debriefing the history of Wu Tang Clan. Ideas for passing the time while crossing the border. A Ted Talk about comforting friends through mourning. She handed the phone back and there was a brief silence, then she gave me a hug. This came as a surprise, so I hesitated, my body remaining neutral as she held me a few seconds then retreated to the balcony where fog was crossing the bay. Eventually, I joined her beside the railing, watching the cars pass on the Coronado bridge.

"Why do we make it so hard to know each other, Sol?"

I liked hearing her say my name. She wiped her nose and eyes with the sleeve of her shirt and took a deep, shaky breath. I lit an imaginary cigarette and held it out to her and she laughed and took it in her fingers and put it to her lips, exhaling a few seconds later. The lights came on again and I tilted my wrist to look at the time and remembered my watch was no longer there and something dark and immense reared its head within me.

"When you transfer your memory to me—will I know it's yours?"

"No—it will become yours."

"How? I already saw the memory—I know it's yours."

"What you saw in the memory happening to me—it will become your memory of what happened to you. Or rather—it will combine with a memory of yours and evolve into something else."

"I never experienced anything remotely close to the thing I chose of yours, though."

"It doesn't matter."

The process is unpredictable, despite our best attempts. Sometimes the input was transformed into a barely recognizable output; sometimes they remained quite close. We could not control for how different people would encode these new memories, but the encoding process always happened in one form or another.

"Sol?"

"Yes?"

"I have something I need to tell you—about the memory of yours I took."

She took a deep breath, trying to slow her breathing.

"I'm not good at apologizing. I don't do it often enough. It's a thing I'm trying to work on." She checked to make sure I was listening. "The memory I took was one of your brother—the one area you told me not to look. I'm sorry. But I want to explain why I did it, okay?"

"Okay."

"I came across memories of your brother, but I wasn't intending on taking any, I honestly wasn't, but I saw one that I know must've caused you a lot of pain and I wanted to—well—I thought maybe if I took that one away and you replaced it with a happy one of me and my brother ... that would be a good thing. Like it was a tumor and you needed surgery. If I fucked up, I'm sorry."

Her eyes welled up. I didn't know whether to continue or if she wanted to talk more, neither of us making any indication to each other.

"The memory I took was when you found him."

"What do you mean?"

"When he died."

"Okay."

She searched my eyes for something she apparently could not

find.

"You don't know what I'm talking about ... do you?"

"I know when he died, but I can't remember how."

"Because I took the memory of how."

She closed her eyes and smoothed out the wrinkles of her shirt, breathing like one about to euthanize a dog.

"Tell me."

She opened her eyes but wouldn't look at me.

"Please tell me."

"I didn't want that to be the last memory you had of him."

"I need you to tell me."

Her eyes were watery and the tone her voice usually had was changed to something I hadn't heard before, something wide open, naked. She finally spoke.

"You knocked on the door, but no one came to open it, so you did. You walked into the apartment and called Jordan's name several times, before sitting on the balcony. It took me until sitting in this chair to realize this was the same apartment. You called his phone and found it ringing on the nightstand next to his wallet. You opened every door in the apartment looking for him ... I still remember the sounds the doors made when you closed them, each one getting louder when you didn't find him. Finally, you went back to the kitchen and found a handwritten note. It said: *I'm sorry to leave you like this."*

It was the first time I'd heard of Jordan apologizing for anything.

"What happened next?"

"You drove around San Diego until you found him. You pulled up to a parking lot that was empty except for one car facing the bay. It was almost nightfall. There was no light in the car, but it was still running and the exhaust was ... piped into the car with him sealed inside."

We waited in the thick silence.

"Anything else from the memory?"

"I'm so sorry."

"I knew he'd died, now I remember how."

"You don't want to talk about it?"

"What is there to talk about?"

She sat back in her chair and looked out the window. I thought about Jordan. Memory Curation was personal for him. He had a pattern of putting too much of himself in his work and that was true with this product—he put his entire self into it.

Nora looked back to me. "Just promise me you'll choose a happy memory of mine to become a happy memory of yours, okay?"

I nodded. Nora curled her hair behind her ears to make space for the gel pads, allowing me to gently adhere each one this time—our faces closer in that moment than they ever had been—the slow pulse of blue igniting when the last one was placed just above her neck.

"Now what?"

"I will launch the program and you will wake up in forty-five minutes."

"Okay."

She shifted in her chair. My finger hovered over the spacebar once more, waiting to initiate the Curation. The laptop's digital timer was all I had to track the time. I missed my watch like a dear friend. I launched the software and dialed Mr. Bray who picked up after Nora had fallen under, shoulders relaxing, head tilting.

"She's under?"

"Yes."

59:47.49

"Good. I will walk you through exactly what to do and you will do exactly what I say. And just so you're aware—all of your assets are frozen."

"What?"

"All of your assets are frozen, darling. If you call law enforcement, they will inform you that your social security number has been used to open bank accounts all over California through which money is being laundered by cartels and they had to freeze your assets while they determine which of your accounts are real and which are not. Now, the *real* reason your assets are frozen is that a colleague in the DEA owes me a favor. Either way, if it goes smoothly tonight, there will be no problem when you wake up tomorrow morning."

"I don't understand."

"Let me put it more simply, darling—I seized all your money. I'm looking after it until you can prove you know how to follow simple instructions. So, let's get on with it."

"I don't get it."

"You're wasting time—Nora is already under. Just do what I tell you to do and everything will be fine. Ignore me and Nora will end up like the old woman you dumped into the back of a truck. Don't think I don't know exactly where she is and how to link her to you. Tell me you will do what I say and that everything will be fine. Say those words."

"I will do what you say and everything will be fine."

"I will tell you where to look and you will describe to me what you see—is that clear?"

"What memory are you looking for?"

"I'm looking for her memory of a funeral with an old, crippled man in attendance. You can go to a specific year, correct?"

"Yes, however, for most people the further back in the person's life the less memories are available. What is the year you are looking for?"

"Fuck knows."

"You don't have an approximate date of the memory, Mr. Bray?"

"Isn't that what I'm paying you for? Search around, it shouldn't take that long. It's a memory of a funeral—how many funerals could she have possible attended?"

"I'm unsure."

"Fucking look then. Try something recent."

"This will take longer to find because the closer we get to present day, the more memories I will have to sort through."

A long sigh came through my headphones. His voice was clear, sounding like he was sitting right beside me.

"Fine. Any better ideas?"

"Whose funeral did she attend? Was it an older relative? A grandparent? An aunt?"

"She's an orphan. The funeral she attended—which she *should* remember—was of another orphan. A kid maybe or an older one, I don't know."

I started with Nora's most recent memories and worked backward, scrolling through this year, pausing over a memory of Nora and Gabe watching the dusk fall over some scarecrows on the estuary and walking Playas de Tijuana at dawn. I dragged this memory into the *Transfer* folder then scrolled to 2039 and scanned the screenful of memories, my eyes darting one to another to another to another—memories of Nora playing dodgeball with kids, talking with older men at bars, fixing a ramp at the skate park, walking alone through dark fields, drinking on rooftops, having sex. Some memories contained a single moment from a day—like witnessing a car being t-boned—and nothing else; others contained a succession of moments strung together—looking up at a pink sky / continuing a jog moving from dirt path to street / passing a dead coyote. Dozens of small moments like this. I could spend hours and not find the funeral Mr. Bray sought.

"The recent memories are too numerous for me to search each one for this funeral, Mr. Bray. Is it possible she attended the funeral in her childhood?"

Silence on the other end, then a shuffling. I waited. Aggravated breathing flowed into my ears.

"It's possible. Recovering the location from an old memory will be more difficult, correct?"

"The location of the cemetery?"

"Yes, that's the whole fucking point—finding where this cemetery is in Tijuana—this place of miracles."

"I don't understand."

"Sol—find a memory of a funeral and tell me every single goddamn detail about it. Understand? Try 20 years ago."

"The timestamps might not be accurate—Creatives lose track of time, so the further back the memory, the more unlikely the timestamp will be accurate."

"Just find it."

32:39.29

Finding a detail in a memory from 20 years ago was like trying to spot a specific person in a marching band from the top of a stadium. I tapped Control-F then typed "2022" and the screen scrolled past clusters of memories, taking me to the line separating 2021 from 2022. One memory spanned both. I hovered over the memory with my cursor and saw fireworks reflecting on the water in a New Year's celebration. I scrolled through the New Year's memory-segments that populated the screen, but that day/night revealed no funeral of any kind. I moved through the memories from 2022, listening to Mr. Bray's rhythmic breathing on the other line, the rise and fall of it like a wave cresting. Nora had several memories from that year—each thumbnailed in front of me with its own preview. I started with the first one, previewing it to find a birthday cake, balloons, etc., so I moved on. In the next one, she stood at a glass pane looking at a gorilla five times her size staring back.

"Tell me what you are looking at right now."

"So far from that year, she remembers a birthday party and a zoo visit. I'm moving on to another memory from 2022."

"From now on you tell me every detail as you see it."

"The third memory is Nora climbing a tree and getting high off the ground and she is scared so a young boy climbs up and helps her down, limb by limb. The fourth memory is a woman cooking over a stove while Nora is trying on the woman's sandals. The fifth memory is—"

21:34.07

"Go back to that memory."

"You want me to describe it again, Mr. Bray?"

"No, darling, I want you to tell me everything you saw in it."

"I did, Mr. Bray. The woman cooking, small Nora, large sandals."

"That's it?"

"Memories are brief, Mr. Bray. I am moving to the next one."

I paused a moment, trying to make sense of what I was seeing in the fifth memory, but continued speaking despite being unsure whether my descriptions were coherent.

"Afternoon. She lines up behind an outdoor sink with kids her age, about six or seven-years-old, each using pellets of laundry detergent to wash their hands then eating sandwiches brought by college students."

"That's all?"

"This is how the process works, Mr. Bray."

"Go quicker. Look for something you can't explain."

My eyes drifted from the computer screen to Nora, her stomach rising with each breath. In the blue light, I noticed a small birthmark behind her ear where her hair had been pulled back; it was the size of a thumb and began at the edge of her sideburn and curled up toward her temple.

"We need to be mindful of time," I said.

"Keep going."

14:18.22

I sorted through the memories of the following year—2023—memories of a woman rubbing her eyes as she read a dense textbook under lamplight. Gabe at a wrestling match, looking down at a boy he'd just defeated. Nora prowling the aisles of a grocery store on her hands and knees and jumping out from behind stacks of vegetables to scare people. I watched Nora getting older through each memory, growing in confidence in ways both large and small—fighting a bully on the playground; intercepting the postman so she could screen the mail; skating in restricted areas. Becoming a person comfortable in every space.

"I am not coming across anything resembling a funeral."

"Why are you so fucking useless?"

"I don't know where to look for what you want."

"Sol—don't make me fire you from my company."

I stopped looking at the screen and looked at Nora instead. I leaned in, noticing small indentations on each side of her eyes that indicated she wore glasses sometimes. She usually never sat still enough for me to notice these things.

"Have you not figured it out?"

"I'm sorry?"

His voice tsk-tsked, mumbling several indiscernible things in my ear as I tried to understand what he was referring to.

"Did you not realize that you've been working for me ever since you started in this trade? I was the first investor, Sol. You think I didn't know where this technology came from? That I just found you out of the blue? I hand-chose you for this assignment because you've proven that you do what you're told. Now find the fucking memory. Look in her childhood."

I said nothing; did not move. The only sound I could hear was his breathing growing louder and I forgot where I was for several moments until I looked upon Nora once more.

"What are you doing?"

"Looking at Nora. I wish you could see how beautiful she is."

"Stay focused."

"I think it's best if we postpone."

"There is no postponing. This must be dealt with now. You can't walk out."

My throat ran dry. I looked at Nora as she sat in the leather chair a few feet from me. Her hair had fallen around her shoulders framing her neck elegantly, swan-like. She felt so far away.

04:49.11

I went back to the end of 2023, where I'd left off, when Nora looked to be eight-years-old. I hurried through memory after memory, looking for any item, any person, that accompanies the setting of a funeral—priests, churches, coffins, etc., until I finally stumbled upon a thumbnail featuring small glowing crosses. I glanced back at the digital timer on top of the laptop—it had turned off. I clicked the Reset button—nothing happened.

"What's going on?"

"The timer—it turned off for some reason."

"Don't worry about the time, I'm monitoring it."

I hesitated. I could close the Curation with a single click.

"Sol—the sooner you find this memory, the sooner this ends."

"I may have found something—but I think we should bring Nora back and return to it a different time because I know where to find it now."

"What is it?"

"I think it's the memory you are looking for."

"Describe it."

"I can at another ti—"

"This is it, Sol, this is the only time we have. Now do you want to transfer this memory or continue wasting what time we have?"

I looked back at the screen—Nora's memory spread before me. A woman in this preview looked familiar somehow. I peered closer trying to discern if the woman I saw was the one I knew but at a younger age.

"There's a woman—with one blue eye and one brown eye."

"This is the one. Now—start from the memory's beginning and describe everything."

"The sky is pink and blue."

"Dusk?"

"Yes."

"Go on..."

The gel pads turned red.

"A baby's small hands, a black coffin. Weeping. Driving east on a freeway—"

"What does the road look like?"

"Too dark to tell. A big mountain covered in lights."

"Is it an urban space or countryside?"

"I don't know."

"Are there lights in the distance?"

"Yes."

"But not close? The cemetery is not close to the lights—the lights are in the distance?"

"Yes."

"Outskirts then. What else? What do you see? Look for street signs, landmarks, directions of any kind."

The gel pads started flashing red.

"The cemetery is on a bluff by the freeway—a bluff on the righthand side."

"Good. What's *in* the cemetery? Describe what you see there.

Describe everything."

"White crosses mark the graves. Voices. People gather around a new hole, holding candles, faces aglow. An old man, barefoot in a wheelchair. He's pushed to the edge of the grave where he—he gets up—"

"Transfer it."

I dragged the thumbnail of the memory to the *Transfer* folder. The hard drive blinked. The flashing accelerated.

"It'd take too long to download. I need to shut down the software and—"

"Complete the transfer, Sol."

I hesitated.

"Sol—we are fine on time. Do it."

I sat back in my chair, the progress bar indicating 45 seconds … 32 … 25 …

I noticed Nora was wearing her brother's softball t-shirt, her stomach rising slightly as she breathed, hands clasped before her.

15 … 12 … 9 … 6 … 3

The red flashing stopped.

Her hands fell to the side.

CHAPTER 11

I sat on the sofa across from Mr. Bray, each of us waiting for the other to say the first word. I placed the hard drive with the memories on the coffee table between us. I had a fever running at 102, and a headache that made me see neon blotches like when you look at the sun. He removed a nail file from his pocket and scraped it across his fingernails. I tried looking out the window, but his floor lamp was on and the window just reflected Mr. Bray and me. He brushed his nails against his shirt, rubbing the dead skin off.

"If you have something to say, say it."

The bookcase behind him felt ornamental, as if each book reinforced whatever its owner said by its mere presence on the shelf.

"Nora might die."

"And whose fault is that?"

"I was doing what you told me to do."

"And that put Nora in a coma."

"You forced me."

"Did I?"

I recounted the events of the previous night in my head—the images of Nora's memories with a voiceover of Mr. Bray's threats spoken from the same seat where he currently sat filing his nails. I thought about how all he needed was a phone; he didn't need to stand over me, didn't need a gunman to coerce me, didn't even need to see me. We looked at each other and he gave a slight nod and, somehow, I knew. It became clear in a single moment.

"You hadn't really frozen my assets."

He smiled, the Venus flytrap opening once more. I felt as if my internal organs had dissolved. His fingers gripped the armrests like a throne.

"I'll tell someone what happened." I said grabbing the hard drive from the table and pocketing it as I walked toward the stairs, pausing at the top step when he started clapping.

"You are a marvel. You do this exact same routine every single time. It's like talking to an Alzheimer's patient. You come here, upset, then make a show of being distraught, then a few months pass and you do the same thing all over again."

"What are you talking about?"

He waved a hand toward himself, beckoning me back. I stayed at the staircase, holding the banister. More neon blotches clouded my vision as I tried to keep him in view before I gave up and closed my eyes and listened to his voice.

"Sol, darling, you are so assiduously naïve that even if I explained everything to you *again* I don't think you'd believe me."

"Explained what?"

"Jesus, here we go."

I walked to the sofa and stood behind it, watching him. His hair was pushed back from his wide forehead which looked like a second face devoid of features. His dark eyebrows had a way of accentuating his expression like bolding text.

"Think about it, Sol, it's not that hard to figure out."

Mr. Bray implied a conclusion I knew but did not acknowledge—the understanding sinking in like watching a wildfire headed for your town.

"I want to hear you say it."

"No."

"Come now, darling, just say it. Don't worry you're not speaking it into existence, it's there whether you say it or not."

My vision was going. I closed my eyes but what I saw did not change very much. A plane descended toward the airport, but I hoped it would steer into the apartment instead.

"Say it."

"Nora was not the first." I said. "We have worked together before."

"Several times. Granted you've never put anyone in a coma, that's a first."

"How many have I curated like this?"

"A lot. Between you and your brother, I've been able to identify all the possible sites of the cemetery. I'm indebted to you both."

"I don't remember the others."

"Of course not. We make sure you don't. Speaking of which" he held his watch up to his ear and it spoke the time. "Paco is on his way."

"What?"

He sighed.

"Listen—we can do this now or later, it doesn't really matter to me, but I promise you it will get done."

"Paco is coming here now?"

Sweat broke out on my forehead anew. I looked from Mr. Bray to the top of the staircase, expecting Paco to be there.

"Any minute."

"How can you do this?"

He weighed this thought in his mind, drumming his fingers along the armrest of his chair as if deliberating on whether to take a hit out on someone.

"Your question, darling, should be how could *we* do this. We. And if I were to address that question of how we could do this, I would have to admit that I see nothing wrong in what we're doing."

"Nora is in a coma. How's that not wrong?"

"Listen, I'm tired of this moralizing, especially from you. But if you insist, then yes, I can play that game. I invite you to think about all the families that have stayed together because someone was able to fulfill their needs by using our service rather than wrecking their marriages and workplaces. Their *selves*. Every person has a self-destructive impulse and we are a vastly better option than them throwing their life away. Think on that, darling. Think of all the people we employed during this process and the money they used to provide for their children. Better to sell their minds than their bodies. Tell me—have we ever paid below market value for these memories?"

"We determine the market for these memories."

"So—what is the answer to my question?"

"No—we have not paid below market value."

"And do these Creatives need this money?"

"Yes, they do."

"And do they sign releases acknowledging the risks of Curation?"

The documentation Mr. Bray referred to was a 56-page document outlining the process in verbose, technical jargon. Section IV/A/3/b has a footnote citing the reality that memories are taken from—and never returned to—the Creative in the following way:

All chanced decisions that could result in being potentially detrimental or adverse for the Creative, are the responsibility of the Creative to understand, and by acquiescing to the binding terms of this contract, the Creative acknowledges these concerns are not the responsibility of JADB or its affiliates. Suboptimal complications can potentially result in adverse impact on quality of life or even, potentially, temporary or untemporary loss of life.

I wrote the waiver in a single day. I was told to make it as expansive as possible because they didn't know what iteration the product was going to take. I doubt it has ever been updated.

"All of this is above board. We're a certified LLC, you've seen your W-2. We purchase and trade memory. And within our organization, this is the process. You know that. You signed your contract. And we have paid Nora fairly for her memories. Her disbursement is currently being delivered to her."

"She didn't know what would happen."

"She signed the contract."

"She didn't read the contract."

"And whose fault is that?"

"I'm going to the police in the morning to tell them everything."

"Fine, go. Everything we are doing is legal."

"She's in a coma because of us."

"She's in a coma because of *you*. This only ends after you've transcribed. And you *will* do so."

"I won't."

He leaned back, running his fingers down the Venetian shades that covered the window to his right. After a minute of this, he moved to the sofa, tapping the seat beside him. He waited patiently as I hesitated for several moments then sat for reasons I still do not understand. My fever worsened, a dampness forming under my eyes. His breath cast a stench around me that was so familiar, a smell that would reside in my memory bank regardless of what Paco would do to me.

"Where are orphans buried when they die? They have no family, therefore no family plot, right? So, what do you do with them?"

"I don't know, Mr. Bray."

"Nora's an orphan. Like her mother before her. And Nora's particular orphanage has its own cemetery, somewhere in Tijuana, where miracles occur—performed by an old cripple who attends each one. Or so the memories indicate. You know, they are in you."

"I don't understand."

"The trouble was that the memories we acquired were of the miracles themselves with only clues as to where the cemetery was—a geographical detail here and there. I had people scour every cemetery in Tijuana—the ones we had pinned and those we hadn't—looking for the miraculous graveyard, attending dozens of funerals, waiting to witness something inexplicable, waiting for the old cripple. None found anything. Don't think I didn't try other methods like questioning every single orphan from this godforsaken place that we could find, but none of them talked. None. And for no amount of money either. Can you imagine that?" He shook his head. "So I had to navigate a different route. And I'd nearly lost hope! Then Nora came along. Your brother found her. He was the one that put this whole network together, tracked down the orphans, the cemeteries. My right hand. He set everything up for you to succeed and you did, you *succeeded*."

The aroma of Mr. Bray, of the apartment, that metallic smell, was suffocating. I laid down on the carpet—the air above me moving like it does when you stare at the dark for too long. He was waiting for me to continue to ask questions, but I did not. I found that not asking the question lessened his satisfaction when giving the answer—the answer he could not refrain from. I realized in that moment that if I kept quiet, Mr. Bray would finish his own thoughts out loud, answer his own questions. He stood up and towered directly above me, his head blocking the light so all I saw was the shadow of his face and the outline of his top-heavy body.

"Why are you so desperate to find this cemetery?" I asked.

"It's the place of miracles, Sol. And I'm running out of time. I have the same pancreatic cancer my mother had—untreatable. But she was saved by a holy man and so will I be."

More images flooded my mind as he stood over me—a baby swaddled in a cardboard box; the feathers of a bird forming a perfect circle in sand; melting plastic to apply over the hole of a shoe—my headache worsening with each one. All I wanted was to leave.

"Get up, it's almost time."

"I don't have to do this."

"You are contractually obligated."

I got up and steadied myself with my hand on the couch until the blotches obscuring my vision evened and I looked at him—an old man whose years had given him a slight hunch he couldn't straighten. My legs were numb. There was a knock at the door.

"Ah, that must be Paco."

The door opened and I turned toward the staircase and waited as the pounding of a foot on each stair got louder until Paco's bald head materialized under the light that hung above the top stair. I looked back at Mr. Bray.

"There is no walking out on this. Even if you were to leave this apartment tonight, we'd simply do it another time, it doesn't matter."

Paco stood at the top of the stairs with his arms at his sides and looked as if he did not know me, had never seen me before, had never drank a beer overlooking Playas de Tijuana with me.

"You still have to transcribe Nora's memory," Mr. Bray said.

The buffalo head in the corner seemed to grow larger in my field of vision, as if he were turning his head from profile to front-facing. Paco frisked me and wrestled the hard drive from my pocket then looked at Mr. Bray who massaged his face casually, scratching the underside of his chin where hair had collected in the places difficult to shave. Paco pointed to the door with the hourglass doorknob and followed behind me. I opened it and saw the desk and the Braille map. Beside these, a wheelchair, a laptop, gel pads with a blue glow.

⧗

I awoke in that same chair with a new memory that consumed my thoughts. A computer booted up. Paco opened the word processor to a blank sheet and told me to type, so I began typing, thinking of the dusk, the triangular mountain, the white crosses on the slope, the angle of the terrain, the topography of the plain below, my fingers transcribing from muscle memory. I kept wiping my eyes because my fever had increased the amount of fluid that seemed to fill them. It took ten minutes to complete. I selected *File*, then *Print*, and listened to the printer hum.

I turned around and noticed something on the wall behind me, opposite the map. I switched on the second light. Stapled in neat rows were transcripts, like the one I'd just made, dotted with lines of Braille directly under each line of printed text. I looked over the transcripts and saw my name atop each one, beside the Creative number. There were a few dozen. I skimmed one then another and another and another and each described a funeral, some similar, others entirely different. The level of detail fluctuated but the emotions were consistent. I looked at the map on the other wall—it had the same number of pins stuck into the paper, pins with little red heads—one pin for each transcript, each memory. The door opened.

"Done?"

Mr. Bray walked forward and felt for the printer until his fingers wrapped around it and slid down to the Brailled paper which he pulled from the tray. He ran his index finger along the lines of dots and smiled.

"Our map is ready for one more pin," he said. "Well done, darling, well done."

I followed Paco into the living room and took a deep breath through my nose, trying to better encode the smell in order to associate it with trauma. I took in the buffalo head, the breeze making the Venetian blinds click, the bookcase, the incense, the shelf with Native American pottery. I turned back to Mr. Bray.

"I want to keep these memories of Nora. Of what I did."

"You can't."

"Why not?"

"We didn't used to wipe the memories of our Curators, but we found that we had to, after your brother's suicide. For some reason, it got to him."

"What did?"

"I haven't the foggiest idea, darling."

I opened my mouth to speak, but Paco shoved me back into the room, closed the door, and locked it behind us. My body shook. It was hard to breathe. I settled into the wheelchair once more, sweat breaking out as I tried looking outside, twisting my neck to look behind me, but there was only darkness. I closed my eyes and made a pact with myself that if Nora died, I would too.

CHAPTER 12

A pair of red Converse hung on the electrical wire across the deck from my apartment. I first noticed them a few weeks ago and they've come to serve as a time marker, the light coloring them differently throughout the day—in the morning, a soft red; at noon, a bright red; at dusk, maroon.

There's a hospital I've been drawn to, the same one I used to visit when I couldn't sleep. Over the last couple weeks, I've walked my dog there several times and sat in the corner of the parking lot looking up at a room—four floors up, three to the left—where a woman lay comatose. Sometimes, at night, I'd see a man's silhouette. He arrived one time while I was there, parking his truck a few yards from where I hid in the bushes. I waited as he got out, locked his car, checked each door handle of his park ranger truck several times and headed toward the entrance of the hospital with a book tucked under his arm. When he came out two hours later, he got in his truck, started the ignition, put his head against the steering wheel and wept. The next night, the room was empty. I haven't seen the park ranger since.

I decided to carhop in the vacant cars that people had paid for but failed to use; the ones that became public transportation on the main routes. My first car terminated at the North Park water tower, which I climbed by wedging my shoe into the crossbars and hoisting each foot up. I swung my leg over the rail of the observation deck and watched the cars roll along El Cajon

Boulevard, listening to a couple on the sidewalk dream up names for their baby beside a homeless woman who arranged a collection of stuffed animals into a tea party. I climbed down after some unknown interval of time and took another prepaid car without looking at the destination and arrived at Chicano Park where murals of Cesar Chavez had been painted on the bellies of freeways. Another car took me to the H Street station in Chula Vista near the trolley where people filtered out from afternoon Mass. A final car took me on the 5-South past tract homes with synthetic lawns and businesses that filled small needs.

The car dropped me at the Jack in the Box next to the pedestrian crossing in San Ysidro where passengers filtered out of the trolley that ended at the same point. I merged with the flow of headphoned teenagers weaving up the ramp toward the pedestrian crossing and passed through customs, always saying the same answer for when they asked what my reason for crossing was—*Just visiting*. The Tijuana River was little more than a green trickle. From the bridge, I could see figures crouching in the irrigation tunnels that fed into the canal, the lucky ones having a tent of their own. One had built a little shelter of cinderblock and plywood and all I saw of him were bare feet catching the last hours of sunlight. The bridge switchbacked before emptying into a plaza mostly devoid of people. I walked toward Avenida Revolución, passing murals and beggars and pharmacies that smelled like disinfectant, the sun behind the two-story buildings which brought shade to my side of the street and sepia toned the other side. Cops drove leisurely by one after another as if on a circuit. Lining each side of the street were novelty shops, bars, cafes, antique stores, markets, leather goods—all selling something you put on your body or in it. Old men chewed on toothpicks, sitting on little stools outside liquor stores they owned, staring at me as I passed, indifferent to whether I bought a bottle of tequila or a Coca-Cola with the glass bottleneck stretched into a swirl.

I took another car onto oil-streaked roundabouts with no clear rules but no accidents either, ending in a road with frequent stoplights where vendors walked the line of cars selling things you didn't want. I merged onto a three-lane highway, the dense network of streets and people and art and food replaced by acres of car dealerships with broken windows and palatial government buildings with empty parking lots. I watched painters rappel down a non-descript building applying dark blue paint one roll at a time. Leaves hung limp from withering palm trees above a shopping center next to an auto mechanic with two pyramids of dusty tires stacked higher than telephone poles. The car continued east.

The road climbed above a baseball field of orange dirt and cinderblock dugouts where a man dragged a shopping cart roped to a tarp. A canyon to the right had a bridge spanning it like the ones built for trains in the Old West, and above one side of the canyon, a quarry with stationary bulldozers and backhoes and loading trucks. On the other side were terraces with varied-colored homes. Rising above it all to the northeast was a mountain with the inscription *JESÚS ES EL SEÑOR* written in huge letters beneath its summit where a half-dozen antennae stood. The mountain looked familiar. Houses and trees and roads began midway down, its top half being mostly featureless. The road crested, dipped, then rose once more. Five minutes later, I glimpsed a small cemetery clumped on the ridge with the northerly aspect overlooking the freeway, high enough that it was mostly hidden from view. I opened the door to make the car pull to the shoulder and once it was stopped, I got out and walked up the dirt road that led to the entrance. As the day closed, the sky diffused in blue and pink color. I sat there, looking at the dirt road that bisected the cemetery. In the distance were hills with conjoined peaks like humps on a camel's back, a full moon between them. Graves clustered in the corner nearest the road as if to watch the cars pass by.

The cemetery was one of three—one for each stratum of society. Lights blinked on above well-trimmed lawns where pristine headstones ornamented the upper-class cemetery a half-mile away; the sound of mariachis loud enough for me to tell its singer was a tenor. I'd heard about how wealthy Mexicans often interred their loved ones in tombs built like studio apartments—complete with air conditioning, a fridge, bar, furniture—but never believed it until I saw several built at the edge of that cemetery, each with a sleek front door and security system.

The middle-class cemetery lacked the opulence but retained the greenery, with aisles of small pines and palm trees. Paths marked by white stones wove through the interior where a few maintenance staff were finishing up their shifts under the streetlamps that yellowed the ground, allowing visitors to find the way back to their cars.

In the lower-class cemetery where I sat, there were only a handful of trees—cypresses and peppertrees—planted beside graves as if they could use the shade. The wind rapped against plastic bags stuck in the bramble that enveloped the barbed wire fence that bordered the cemetery. Broken pottery, empty Fanta bottles, garbage bags, teddy bears, and shattered glass littered the uneven rows of graves. The adjacent ridge was covered with blackened soil right up to the cemetery, stopping at the fence line—the fire, apparently, respecting the dead.

There was one corner of it that stood apart from the rest—furthest from the entrance road. Tire marks from a truck or some vehicle with thick tread led up to an embankment where lumps rose from the dirt. Beside these, two shovels that acted as paperweights for burlap sacks tucked under them. Someone had affixed a small sign to a wooden pole in front of these lumps, the sign having no words, only the shape of an hourglass.

As the night descended, the sky turned purple and the crosses glowed like little moons. I sensed movement and walked to where the sound was coming from and saw a figure hidden by one of the few peppertrees in the first row of graves beside the freeway. It was an old man in a wheelchair reaching for the headstone of the nearest grave—leaning forward as far as he could, just far enough so his fingertips touched the top of the wooden cross that had *Maria* painted across it with the birth date *8/21/2001* and the death date peeled away except for the year, *2001*.

The old man finished his prayer and looked at me as if he had been expecting me. In the dying light I could see his bare feet. I took the handles of his wheelchair and rolled him to the next grave in the row where I watched as he leaned forward and touched a headstone. In front of the headstone was a fenced space where sunflowers, roses, daisies, and chrysanthemums grew. The old man closed his eyes and mumbled a prayer and all I could see were the outline of his profile, the movement of his lips. He finished and pointed to the next grave. This one had the birth and death as the same date. In front of the headstone was a circle of rocks the length and width of a small child and inside the circle was a rubber dinosaur, a toy car, Mickey Mouse, all bleached from the elements. The headstone was just out of reach so I locked the brakes of the wheelchair and put a hand under his belly and another on his back so that he could lean further out of his seat to touch the cross and say whatever he needed to say. I watched his eyebrows bend with contemplative prayers as we kept going down the line—a grave like a brick pizza oven; a pink cross; a cross with cherubim; one with a wreath; one with the name faded; one with the number 38 and nothing else.

When he finished praying, an orange light appeared at the

entrance. The light seemed to approach by itself, unattached, floating along the night. When it finally drew close, it revealed itself as a lantern held by a ten-year-old boy. He wore a hand-me-down sweatshirt that said the name of a high school, sleeves engulfing his arms.

"Howdy," the boy said.

He wore a primary-colored hat and rubber shoes. The boy told me to follow him, lantern in hand, and I did while the grandfather watched us. He started collecting wood that was scattered throughout the graveyard, mostly jagged pieces broken off from palettes. Pieces of bedframes—slats connected by a thin rope and a headboard cloven in two—lay in a heap near the brush. We gathered a few armloads and made a pile where the dirt paths converged. I went to retrieve the old man who had gone back to praying amid the graves. He was parked in front of one which looked new—the headstone was immaculate and the flowers fresh. He lit four candles and placed them at each corner of the grave, hands clasped in a moment of rapture while he spoke each word as if it might bring her back. I looked at the name on the headstone.

NORA RINCÓN
2/12/2014 - 28/11/2040
Descansando en el lugar de los Milagros.

There was a skateboard, a paperback, and a pair of Converse in front of the headstone surrounded by flowers. A framed photo of her leaned against the stone, lighted by a candle. She was beautiful.

"Did you know her?" I asked.

"Yes."

The boy ignited the bonfire with a cigarette lighter and told us to come over. The temperature dropped as the night settled in. I sat across from them, quiet, the flames of the bonfire licking the air, a slight breeze sending the smoke toward the mountain behind me where hundreds of lights had given the foot of the mountain a sequined shoe. The wheelchair's plastic squares that held his bare feet in place were melted at the near edge. His eyes were the color of worn leather in the firelight.

"What does the inscription on that woman's grave mean?"

"*Descansando en el lugar de los Milagros*—'Resting in the place of miracles'."

"Miracles happen here?"

He nodded.

A memory floated to the front of my mind, one of a barefooted man standing up from his wheelchair to drop dirt in a grave. The boy and the old man both stared at me, but in the darkness, I couldn't see their expression.

"I've been coming here to pray for fifty years and never seen a gringo. And now I've seen two in two weeks."

"Who was the other?"

"A blind man my age. He came to the memorial seeking healing."

"Was he healed?"

"Of course not. That is not the type of miracle that occurs here."

The moon continued to rise, appearing smaller as it climbed the night sky and the fire settled down as the remaining wood turned to embers that glimmered bright red around the edges. In the distance, coyotes called to one another; cars became fewer and fewer. The old man looked at me again and reached over and laid a hand on my forehead and prayed in an unknown language I couldn't understand. When he was done, he smiled then said goodbye and the boy pushed the old man up the slope toward the entrance, singing a ballad together that sounded like one passed down and a rush of memories flooded my mind, as if they were behind a dam that the song broke, but I could not tell which were mine and which were not and perhaps that would always be the case when I recalled a body in a burlap sack, a man wearing a gas mask, a blue horse, a flare arcing above a plain, digits on a timer, the sway of a sun dress, cubicles through a window, a rattlesnake gliding on the ground, dogs looking on from a roof, ocean swimming, water rising, a young man shaving his head, crosses strewn with old clothes and on and on.

THE END

Acknowledgments

Alan Bilton—thank you for serving as my Ph.D. supervisor and believing in this book enough to publish it.

Carole Hailey—thank you for your thoughtful edits and for publishing this book.

Glen Brown, Margarita Pintado-Burgos, Tyler Keevil—thank you for taking the time to read this book and for praising it via blurb, which will hopefully convince some readers to take the plunge. I will forward all disgruntled emails from unsatisfied readers directly to each of you.

Jon Doyle and Glen Brown (yet again)—thank you for reading earlier iterations of this book and giving wise narrative advice.

My teachers: Ellen Manchester, Sean Pierce, and Michael Clark—thank you for helping me discover my voice and aptitude as a writer.

My parents, Bill and Sarah Matthews—thanks for your encouragement and support, emotionally and financially. Wise souls, you are.

Also published by Watermark Press

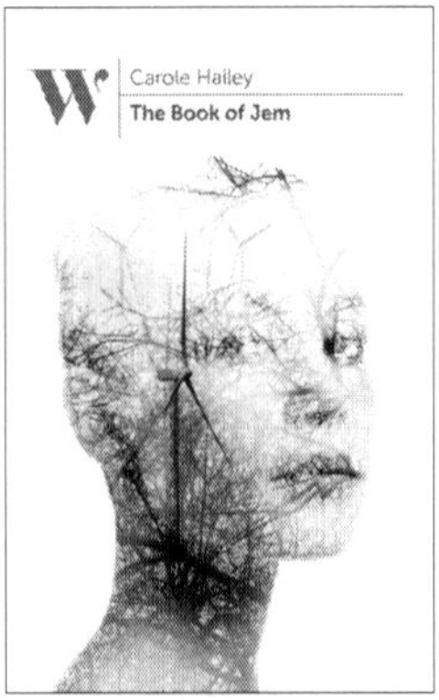

Carole Hailey
The Book of Jem

In the aftermath of catastrophic religious wars, God has been banned.

As snow begins to fall, a young woman – Jem – arrives in Underhill. The isolated community offers her shelter, unwittingly unleashing events that threaten their very existence.

Jem announces that she has been sent to Underhill by God to prepare the villagers to fulfil a devastating purpose. Some believe she is a prophet and defy the law to join her God's Threads religion. Others are certain she is lying.

With their fragile community beginning to fracture, Eileen, the first and most devoted of the believers, decides to record the birth of this new religion in her own Book of Jem.

As God's Threads gather for the apocalypse, the words Eileen has written will determine the fate of Underhill and, ultimately, of Jem herself. But can Eileen be trusted to tell the truth? And how can anyone know what to believe?

'Bold storytelling, with the satirical force of Naomi Alderman's *The Power* but its own claustrophobic sense of place.'
Francis Spufford, author of *Golden Hill*

Alan Bilton
The End of the Yellow House

Central Russia, the black earth forest, near Voronezh, 1919. As the civil war rages, White forces, accompanied by feared Cossack divisions, advance ever closer to Moscow. In the chaos, the Yellow House, a sanatorium at Bezumiye, becomes cut off, the superintendent found murdered, a strange black box atop his head.

As the distinction between doctors and 'guests' frays, the murder sets in motion a nightmarish series of events involving mysterious experiments, the secret police, the Tsar's double, prophetic dreams, giant corpses, possessed cats, sorcery, and the overwhelming madness of war. Into this dangerously combustible mix, a ragged and eccentric police officer arrives, calling himself Inspector Tutyshkin and claiming he has travelled to the house to investigate the superintendent's suspicious demise.

But in this strange game of madness, doubles and disguises, are any of the players truly who they seem?

'A bold and confident novel that throws us into the deep end of post-revolutionary Russian life with fervour and wit. There are knowing nods to Gogol and Bulgakov but the voice is entirely original, with a gem of a phrase on every page.'

MARK BLAYNEY

'A brutal, but often witty and tender tale, *The End of the Yellow House* is a twistedly brilliant emotional rollercoaster.'

DAVID TOWSEY

Carolyn Lewis

Some Sort of Twilight

These twelve stories are of people unsure of their place in the world – Cassie who discovers she can fly and has no-one to tell, Christine who's been in her friend's shadow for a long time, Bernard who loses his job through no fault of his own and Hannah who knows her father is waiting for her to sort his life out.

These stories combine pathos, humour and wisdom to explore how the ordinary can be strange, heartbreaking or comic, illuminating the inner lives of people who feel in some way they're on the edge of their own lives.

Carolyn's stories are a joy to read. Her characters are so perfectly formed that we feel we have always known them. Of course people collect coat hangers! Who doesn't one day find they can fly? Her empathy for them all shines through and we feel in very safe hands

SALLY BRAMLEY, WINNER 2021 CALEDONIA NOVEL PRIZE.